IN

Introduction	Editor's Forward
Chapters	
One	London
Two	London
Three	Vienna
Four	Egypt/Middle East
Five	London
Six	Berlin
Seven	Rome, Argentina
Eight	South Africa
Nine	Washington DC
Ten	Atlanta
Eleven	Kroonstadt
Twelve	Cancun
Thirteen	Santa Elena
Fourteen	Belize
Fifteen	Lima, Peru

Sixteen	Patagonia/Egypt
Seventeen	Chile/ Argentina
Eighteen	Bairloche /Inalco
Nineteen	Andes / Chile
Twenty	Inalco & Chamber
Twenty One	San Martin de los Andes
Twenty Two	Argentina -Washington DC
Twenty three	Barbadoss
Twenty Four	London
Twenty Five	Conclusion

List of characters and references

Foreward

The following novel, which I hope you enjoy, is a mixture of both fact and fiction and where appropriate the actual recorded events in respect of German operations in the Middle East and during the collapse of the Third Reich are shown wherever relevant to the story.

The places visited during the investigation into the neo-Nazi activities and finances do exist but obviously some names and personal activities are ficticious and do not reflect on anyone who may have the same or a similar name.

I decided to write this, my first novel, basing it on my experiences in the investigation of financial crime and other dishonesty plus a long held interest with the events of 1945 and the events that took place in Hitler's bunker.

Subsequently then being personally involved in the investigation of Holocaust denial merchants, terrorist funding and lecturing on money laundering, my first book The Money Launderers was published in 2001 followed by a second edition a few years later.

Recently Amazon KDP published my short autobiography/ cookbook, "The Autobiographical Investigator Cookbook" (not selling very many but a good experience in putting pen to paper)

Olivia

hope you enjoy

Bob B

Obviously there was the need to carry out considerable research while writing this story and a list of some of the reference sources are shown as an Appendix.

The various Hotels, Pubs, and Restaurant/ Bars mentioned do in fact exist but I have only visited a few of them. Rebecca, the beautiful woman in the story is based on all the beautiful women that I have known in my life and she is an amalgamation of Lynda, Paulette, Joy, Liz, Sandra and those who I may be lucky to meet in the future.

Bob Blunden

Suffolk

March 2014

THE SKULL

Chapter One   Day One - London

The phone rang early one Saturday morning and a voice from my past asked for an urgent meet at a small café in Finchley, the Holocaust denial merchants and Neo –Nazis were apparently at it again. The question was, could I do the business again? Only this time put them out of business permanently and put them to sleep in a proverbial sense, not literally.

I arrived at the café early, ordered an espresso and sat outside lighting up yet another coffin nail despite my constant promises to give the habit up. The current copy of the tabloid newspaper, The Sun, lay on the table and a quick look at their page 3 girl, and the latest news about Arsenal Football Club was almost enough reading material for the day, when I caught site of an article about Hitler's skull. It was reported that DNA tests by some American scientist allegedly show that the piece of skull held by the Russians since 1945 was that of a woman. Now come on, "woman?" So this little Austrian Corporal was a female dressed as a man, or was something more sinister coming out of the woodwork. I could see all of the conspiracy theorists having a field day, you know "Hitler is alive and working in Tesco's or Walmart as a check out girl".

My memory bank slipped into the past when as a young boy, I, along with my schoolmates (one who had allegedly set fire to our school in Woodford), had been bussed to an old (2nd World War) rat infested prisoner of war camp on Chingford Plain in Epping Forest where the old prisoner accommodation huts were use as classrooms. My best friend swore blind that there was a man with a little moustache at the back of the classroom who was always putting his right hand up first when the teacher asked a question.

My thoughts were disturbed by Simon, the man from the past, who sat down, shook my hand and got down to business immediately. " As you know Harry there has been a considerable rise in neo-Nazi activity throughout Europe and we have established that someone is providing considerable funding of these groups enabling them to re-start their physical attacks on the Jewish people and also spreading misinformation about recent history. "

I replied "Yes mate, I've heard about this problem in Europe and the extremism that appears to blossoming everywhere."

"Anyway Harry we would like you to establish the source of this new substantial funding and if possible, find out their agenda and help us close them down. Also prepare appropriate evidence that we can use in a Court to get rid of these troublesome people. Hopefully they will then give up and retire to some hidden place preferably under the proverbial rock. "

The owner of the café came out to clear the adjoining table and his mobile phone rang. I noticed him answer the call but did not see him taking a photograph of Simon and myself. He returned inside the café and sent the photograph to a man sitting in an Audi car parked in a Vienna side street.

After discussing some of the latest developments in the UK and Europe I agreed with Simon's request and we shook hands and he left the café.

The current situation in the Middle East was obviously causing considerable concern with the news that the mad Mullahs in Iran were getting near to having their own nuclear weapons, the Fascist Muslim Brotherhood had been thrown out of the Egyptian Government and listed as a terrorist organisation plus chaos prevailed everywhere. The additional concern was whether there was a hidden agenda somewhere?

On returning to my office I opened up the various websites that catered for these extremists and analysed those that had provision for donations to be made to support their crackpot ideas. Our known targets had set up the provision for donations in North and South America, United Kingdom, Germany and Mexico. Mexico? This was certainly new as previously only the former jurisdictions had been used by these people. The idiots who had made donations to these funds never realised that the money had previously been used to support a personal, comfortable and sometimes extravagant lifestyle. The other sites I found tended to be localised but covered most West European countries. One site that certainly grabbed my attention was a new website in Brazil as this country had been the hiding place of some 4,000 Nazis who had fled there at the end of the war to escape the hangman's noose.

Brazil, this was strange as the information appeared to be in conflict with history as they entered the war on our side late in the conflict. Argentina, yes as it was to where many of the notorious scumbags like Mengele and Eichmann had fled to, but Brazil? Why did they allow so many Nazis in at the end of the war?

A number of computer messages to my network of contacts in Europe and America initiated small payments by cheque to our target's various sites, plus the Mexican, Brazilian, Italian, Spanish and other websites.

Chapter Two -   Day Six to Day Twelve

A few days later, my examination of the cleared cheques revealed details of the various bank accounts where the donations had ended up. It was now time to use those individuals who know someone somewhere who can open bank accounts anywhere in the world. This is not fiction and like everything on this planet, all is possible at a price.

I was now impatient for these results and after what seemed an inordinate amount of time I met one of my "well connected" individuals in L'Autre, a small Polish/Mexican restaurant in Shepherds Market, Mayfair. The Canadian proprietor shook my hand; "Nice to you Harry, it's been a long time. Are you still drinking that Polish Bison Grass Vodka and getting smashed?"

" No you cheeky sod that was ages ago when I was chatting up that private banker to find out whether the money stolen in Bombay had gone through the private bank round the corner that she worked for."

Anyway I exchanged envelopes with my contact and during our conversation over Polish Sausage and Mexican beer about the state of the country including a rant about jobsworths, politicians and bank managers, my "connected" man told me about the high turnover of money going through the Brazilian and Mexican bank accounts. There was no doubt that this meant that other accounts would have to be opened to trace these funds from source to final destination. However Mexico was a new one, yes we all know that it is now the pipeline for South American drugs into the USA and corruption is endemic in Mexico but the big question was whether these Neo-Nazis were raising funds by getting involved in the drug trade?

The next few days were spent scheduling and collating the contents of the envelope. To summarise; my various target's accounts showed not only small deposits from what appeared to be individuals but some substantial wire transfers between the jurisdictions where they had accounts and most important of all transfers from banks in Brazil and Argentina through the Mexico bank's account fund.

This meant I needed answers to the following questions;

- Who controlled these accounts?
- What was the source of the funds?
- What was their agenda?
- What was the Mexican involvement?

My "well connected" individual now needed to open these accounts or contact associates in those countries to investigate possibilities. I telephoned him and he told me that it would take a few days.

I arranged to meet Simon to see what his organisation could tell me about Mexico, Brazil, and Argentina. The next phone call was to arrange a flight to

Vienna to visit the Simon Weisenthal centre in Vienna where I hoped to obtain more intelligence about South America.

From my friend's research into Nazi money laundering for his book "The Money Launderers" I knew that during the war, and immediately after, looted money, gold and treasures had been laundered through Switzerland, Italy (the Vatican Bank) and there was speculation that the Government of the Peron's in Argentina was funded by the Nazis, many whom had fled to South America.

In fact the Peron's provided ODESSA with 10,000 blank Argentinian passports for substantial payments. There had also been considerable German activity post war in the Middle East to support and continue the fight against the Jews in the new state of Israel.

Chapter Three – Day Thirteen/Fourteen   Vienna

I met Simon again at the Finchley café where I outlined my need for all the intelligence his organisation had on anti-semetic problems and neo-Nazi groups in South and Central America. He promised to let me have all that they knew within the next week. I advised him that I was off to Vienna and would be in touch on my return, probably within the next few days.

As soon as we left the café the proprietor was making a call on his phone.

I then drove across London and caught a train from Liverpool Street Station to Stansted Airport where I boarded one of the low cost airline's flying cattle trucks (excuse the pun) for Vienna.

On arrival at Vienna airport, I purchased a disposable pay as you go cellphone, grabbed a taxi and we headed for the town centre. Looking out of the rear window I noted a taxi had pulled out behind mine and was following us into town. Now you may think that I am a bit paranoid but an empty cab is either on a mission or finishing work for the day. I signalled the taxi driver to pull in outside the Hotel Belvedere. The taxi following pulled in a few yards back. Paying the driver I walked into the hotel and immediately left by the rear entrance walking through to Baeurnmarkt and booking into City Hotel. It was too late to telephone the Weisenthal centre so I spent an hour checking e.mails for the latest messages and possible intelligence. My body clock told me it was time for a beer so it was off to Dino's Bar in Innere Stadt to check up on the local news.

I found a table in the corner facing the bar entrance and sat drinking a good cold Hopfen Konig beer. Glancing at a newspaper on the next table old Adolf's face stared fanatically from the front page. My German is quite limited but it was obviously yet another article about Hitler's skull. This was probably very topical in Vienna, Hitler, being the local boy who made bad.

I decided to return to the hotel and after checking for any possible strangers, who may have been watching or following me, I walked a constant back tracking roundabout route to the hotel. The following morning I took a couple of taxis to the Simon Weisenthal Centre in Salztorgasse.

I did not notice the Audi parked opposite the Centre as I rang the intercom to gain access to the building.

A very attractive receptionist showed me through to one of the directors offices where I explained to the Director what I was doing and hoped to establish from the Centre's records. He said that he needed to check me out before agreeing to such a request so I gave him my client's details in London and he left the room.

Several minutes later a very attractive blonde haired woman entered the room and asked me to follow her. We then entered a vast library of books and filing cabinets she told me that I could use the writing desk and computer for my research and gave me the various index reference files from where I could locate any of the files I thought that I may need. She also explained that I would need a personal password to authorise the downloading of any information. She leant over me, (very disconcerting) and quickly entered some alpha, numerics on the keyboard and, hey presto, I had complete access. She smiled and left the library..

These files, microfilms, optical discs and computer files provided me with a number of leads especially about the Odessa connection with South America. I also soon discovered intelligence reports on those known active extremist groups operating in South America. What was surprising was there was little mention of Mexico except for the well-known connection between the Mexican drug barons and the South American drug cartels.

What I also found to be very interesting, was the fact that the US Government had only, until very recently, released a large number of secret documents (8 million) about the Nazis. These documents could provide some important leads as a review found on the internet showed a considerable amount of detail in respect of the Nazi's activities after the war with notes of interviews of various of Hitler's staff who were in the Berlin Fuhrerbunker at the end of the Third Reich. These documents could be found at the U.S. National Archives and Records Administration. Apparently the records had previously been kept at Fort Meade, Maryland by the U.S. Army. Unfortunately many had been destroyed, some of the microfilms had deteriorated and apparently it will be years before all of these are available for public consumption.

I could not help thinking of the reports that I recently read about Hitler's Skull so when I read about the interrogation of his secretary, Gertrude Junge, during which she stated that on April 29 1945, she had transcribed Hitler's last Will and Testament just prior to his suicide it certainly got me wondering.

The U.S. intelligence had also noted that Hitler's chauffeur, Kemka, had claimed that on April 29, 1945, he had apparently witnessed the death of Martin Bormann by Soviet gunfire while in an armoured car crossing the Weidendamm Bridge in Berlin, although for many years it had been believed Bormann had escaped to Argentina in South America. It seemed that every year or so after the war there were reports of some Nazi found working and or living wherever.

As for those Nazis who had fled abroad there was details about the Eichmann arrest in Austria where he had impersonated someone else, initially as an Otto Eckmann, but then he changed his name on release to an Otto Henninger, before fleeing to Argentina via Italy, allegedly travelling on an International Red Cross Passport supplied by the pro-Nazi Bishop at the Vatican.

(Note: The German Intelligence Agency BND apparently still has 4,500 pages of classified documents on Eichmann)

During my examination of what was becoming a thrombosis of information the Nazi involvement with the Middle East also reared its very ugly head such as details of the alliance with The Grand Mufti of Jerusalem, Amin el Husseini and Raschid Ali El Gailani , the former Premier of Iraq,(who had joined the Mufti in Berlin from 1941 to 1945), after a failed coup in Iraq.

The pair had, from Berlin, allied themselves to the Nazis, were paid considerable salaries (some in excess of those paid to senior German government officials) and still having the ultimate joint aim to rid Palestine and the Middle East of all Jews. Documents also showed that on November 28, 1941, Hitler actually discussed this aim with Husseini during a meeting at the Reich Chancellery and there were even photographs of Husseini visiting Auchswitz.

I also discovered that the CIA had identified a ring of ex-Nazi SS, and Arabs, the Germans/Austrian element including a number of various individuals including a Biesner, who controlled the group, another named as Wilhelm, Otto Skorzeny (infamous for rescuing Mussolini, dressing up SS troops as American soldiers (MPs) during the Battle of the Bulge and subsequently running ODESSA from Spain after the war) , others including Rademacher, Brunner and Remer. This group were working with the Grand Mufti, and a number of individuals including Halim, Nasser (who took over the Suez Canal in the early 1950's), Sadat (another Egyptian President) plus other Egyptians and Arabs.

Rademacher, who had fled to Syria after the war, was allegedly helped by the West German Politician, Adenauer and a Gestapo Chief, Mildner, who also went to Argentina to join Eichmann

Besides ODESSA, an organisation that most people already knew a little about because of the Hollywood movie; The Odessa File, a couple of other groups came out of the proverbial woodwork.

The Bruderschaft, a group of German military persons, including some very famous WW2 General Staff officers such as Heinz Guderian, (the Panzer expert), and others, all with a common aim to restore the might of Germany.

The other group Spider (Spinne) was also news to me, apparently run by an Austrian, Dr.Johanne Leers, who had been the Nazi Propaganda Minister Goebbels' number two. This group coordinated the movements of Nazis from Germany to the Middle East, South Africa and elsewhere.

After recording the important information on my laptop and sending it encrypted to my office I decided that, as my head was now spinning with all of this information that I had analysed, I'd had enough for the day.

As I left the beautiful blonde woman who had shown me the library let me out of the Centre and as we shook hands she passed a slip of paper into my hand. While driving back to the hotel in the taxi I saw that it had a telephone number written on it. The Audi had pulled out behind my taxi and followed me back into the centre of town.

My phone call to the number on the slip of paper was answered by a female voice that I immediately recognised as the blonde. She asked if we could meet so I suggested Dino's American Bar later that evening. I agreed mainly because I relished the idea of meeting this beautiful woman in a more casual environment.

I must admit that when she arrived at the bar the appearance of an office secretary had vanished, instead was a very beautiful woman wearing a dark blue leather jacket, light blue cashmere sweater, tight designer jeans and expensive leather boots. She walked across the bar floor like a catwalk model and sat down opposite me at the rear of the wood panelled bar.

After ordering her a drink I asked, "Why did you wish to meet me? Surely not a date or is it or am I one lucky bastard?"

She smiled, "Why did you not ask me for my name?"

"Your name is Ingrid as that is what it said on your office door at the centre".

She laughed, "No it's not, it's Rebecca and I'm interested in the reasons for your visit as perhaps there is some information that I am privy to that may be useful to you."

By this time I had noticed a tall well-built man who had entered the bar a few seconds after Ingrid (Rebecca) had arrived and was now sitting a few tables away from us and reading the bar price list as though it was a new best seller. As he was the only single guy in the place he stuck out like the proverbial sore thumb.

She opened her purse and slid a laminated card across the table. It was an ID showing a photograph of Ingrid but the name Rebecca Sherbonne. The card claimed that she was the Austrian Branch director of Exodus gmbh, a subsidiary of an Israeli Travel Agency registered in Tel Aviv. A member of Mossad, the Israeli Secret Service was more likely.

So what did these people wish to discuss with me or were they just being nosy?

Rebecca then said "We had checked you out after your meeting with your client in Finchley, London. We understand that you are trying to establish the reason for the sudden surge of funding to the various neo-Nazi groups. My colleagues are very concerned that you might tread on our toes in respect of an on-going operation especially with the surge of Neo-Nazism in Germany and Eastern Europe. Anyway Harry if we can help you we will but, if we did you would have to keep us up to date with any discoveries that you make and how you intend to develop your investigations."

I replied, "Rebecca what you have just told me is an indication that you are a member of Mossad not some dodgy travel agency."

Again the beautiful smile and she just winked at me.

"Look Harry your enquiries will probably lead you to both South America and the Middle East as after the war some 5,000 Nazis had fled to Argentina, 2,000 to Brazil, 1,000 to Chile and a number to Paraguay and Uruguay. After that a further 20,000 Germans had settled in Brazil between 1945 and 1959 according to the records of Arquivo Historico in Brazil. "

"Yes OK Rebecca, I have noted that the Perons sold Odessa some 10,000 blank Argentinian passports and that a German pro-Nazi Bishop at the Vatican had also provided 800, mainly International, Red Cross Passports, to senior Nazis such as Eichmann and Mengele. "

She half smiled; "You appear to have done some homework Harry".

I smiled, offered her another drink, and then asked her "What do you know about Mexico?"

" Not very much Harry although initially during the war the country had been used as a bolt hole by Nazi spies fleeing from the FBI in the USA and that there was a long established German community in the country just across the border from Texas."

We then continued the discussion over a few more drinks and I noticed that the strange man was still reading the bar menu so I asked her whether her friend should join us. She glanced at the man, whispered to me; "I do not know him." With that I advised her to go to the washrooms and wait for me by the emergency exit door. A few minutes later I followed her and we left the bar through the emergency exit at the rear of the building.

Luckily a taxi was parked in the nearby Concordia Platz and I pushed Rebecca into the taxi instructing the driver to take us away as quickly as he could and we drove off just as the stranger emerged from the bar, appearing to fumble for something in his jacket. A few minutes later we arrived at a small side street restaurant which Rebecca assured me was pretty good and we quickly entered grabbing a table away from the front door and the street.

After ordering a meal and a bottle of wine the big question was who was the man and what was it all about? Rebecca then made a phone call, obviously to one of her contacts but whatever she said I did not know as the language spoken sounded like Yiddish it certainly wasn't German. She finished the call and told me that a team were on the way to check out the mysterious man and she had been instructed to accompany me while I continued my investigations.

Although happy to be accompanied by this very beautiful woman I certainly did not wish this to cramp my style as an individual working alone can often blend into the background easier than two people especially one who attracted admiring stares. "Do you think that is a good idea Rebecca?"

Rebecca just laughed; "We will just have to make out that we are a couple of lovers on honeymoon."

This beautiful woman was certainly beginning to distract me but in the background of my mind were the incidents that had taken place up to this point of time. Why had Mossad or whoever staked me out at Finchley? Who had followed me from the airport? Who was the man in the bar?

After finishing the meal we jumped into a taxi and then boarded a train at the Westbanhof leaving Vienna by express for Bratislava in Slovakia. During the rail journey I managed to book a late flight out of Slovakia back to Manchester in the UK. A quick dash through the airport with few minutes to spare we boarded the aircraft and within minutes after take- off Rebecca had fallen asleep with her head resting on my shoulder. On landing at Manchester we booked a room at Bewley's Hotel and collapsed on our beds after booking an early morning call to get the train to London. Early the following morning we caught the Inter City Express to London arriving at Euston Station just after 9 am.

Chapter Four – 1944 Egypt / Turkey

Authors Note: This chapter is about the downfall of the Third Reich based on historical fact, rumour and supposition plus fiction as to what could have happened.

1942/3/4 were the years that it all became apparent that the Third Reich was beginning to fall apart, Irwin Rommel and his Afrika Korps had stalled in the North African desert and General Paulus and the 6th Army were caught in a trap and were being surrounded by the Russian Army at Stalingrad.

In North Africa the Abwehr had earlier launched Operation Kondor in support of Rommel, the aim of this mission was to infiltrate British Army Headquarters and try to discover the Eighth Army's battle plans.

Joseph Eppler/Hussein Gaafar, a man with dual nationality, his parents being German although he had been raised in Cairo and his mother marrying an Egyptian after his father had died. Fluent in German, English and Arabic he was the ideal spy who, after being recruited and trained by the Germans, he was sent to Cairo by Rommel guided by the Hungarian aristocrat and explorer, Laszlo Almasy. Unfortunately a British Army intelligence officer Major "Sammy" Sanson uncovered the clandestine operation and the Germans were fed false intelligence before the agents were arrested.

Cairo in those wartime days was a hotbed of intrigue with various political and militant factions many of whom wished to get rid of the British from Egypt. Some of the individuals involved in this intrigue subsequently became household names like Anwar Sadat who was a future president of Egypt, and Nasser who in the early 50's having disposed of King Farouk nationalised the British/French Suez Canal.

Athens May 1944

On the edge of the Hellenikon airfield on the outskirts of Athens a group of Greek resistance (EDES) fighters watched as a large aircraft was pulled out of a hangar. To their amazement they saw that it was an American Boeing B17 Flying Fortress with Luftwaffe markings but still carrying an American serial number 42-30048 (later to be identified as Flak Dancer of the 384th Bomber Group USAAF) The captured aircraft was one of many operated by Kampfgeschwader 200, the Luftwaffe's special operations squadron. The four Wright Cyclones started up and the aircraft moved towards the runway. A few minutes later it became airborne and disappeared to the East.

Fact USAAF B.17 serial number 42-30048 Flak Dancer of the 384th Bomber Group USAAF was captured and operated by KG200.

The EDES contacted their controllers and relayed the information about this strange American aircraft.

On board and unknown to those who had watched the aircraft's departure were four special agents, two were Palestinian members of the Muslim Brotherhood who were being controlled by the Grand Mufti's Berlin operation supervised by both the Abwehr and Martin Bormann, the other two were German Abwehr operatives directly controlled by Admiral Canaris.

The aircraft entered Turkish airspace and then turned South towards the British Protectorate of Palestine. The pilot, Hans

Fittmann, an experienced bomber aviator who had flown with the Luftwaffe in Spain (Condor Legion) Poland, over London, Coventry and Russia, throttled back and glanced at the shape of a Focke Wulf 190 that had appeared on his port wing. He waved and the fighter pilot returned his salute then peeled off disappearing into the distance. The aircraft was obviously one of the aircraft supplied by the Reich to Turkey in an attempt to keep that country out of the war. Hans turned to his co-pilot, a young Bavarian who was still new to combat flying but a very natural aviator, "the sooner we get this mission over the better ", and increased the throttles pulling back on the controls until levelling off at some 1000 ft above Palestine.

The navigator radioed that they were 10 minutes from Ein Arik and the two Palestinians were checked to ensure that their parachutes were secure. A few minutes later the bomb doors opened, the aircraft being filled with warm desert air and the roar of the engines.

On the ground two beacons were lit as the sound of the approaching aircraft could be heard. Hans throttled back for a moment and made a chopping sign with his right hand indicating that the two men should jump. Both disappeared into the night sky as the bomb doors closed and the aircraft increased speed descending to a very low height of some 100 ft.

Ein Arik   British Palestine Protectorate

Site of the tallest minaret in Palestine the two men landed in an orange grove a couple of kilometres from the settlement.

They were met by half a dozen Palestinians who helped them out of their parachutes and into a small truck which was then driven off towards a local farm. On arrival at the farm they greeted two individuals, one a Syrian in army uniform and a German civilian. The papers, cases and files that they had carried from Berlin were handed over and refreshments of coffee and dates were carried into the room from the small kitchen.

The German, a member of the SS working for Walter Schellenberg, opened a case and sent a radio message confirming the contacts and receipt of the files. Some of the cases contained £10,000,000 in forged British notes, the others gold ingots worth $2 million.

Egypt

The B17 continued flying South crossing the Mediterranean and the Egyptian coast to the East of Alexandria and then circling Cairo before heading towards the Al Farafrah Oasis in the desert.

Two small beacons could be seen and Hans throttled back, dropped the flaps and the aircraft descended and landed on a compressed sand runway.

Hans muttered; "My God – this place is still a shit hole "as the aircraft bumped across the uneven sand and rocks before coming to a halt. A year previously he had dropped some equipment and KG200 technicians at this temporary airstrip during Operation Dora who were subsequently lucky to escape the attentions of Free French and British units that had, after the interrogation of a captured German spy in Freetown, Sierra Leone, raided the airstrip and captured equipment but failed to capture the KG200 technicians.

Hans kept the engines running as the two German agents left the aircraft and their "luggage "was offloaded. He turned the aircraft into the wind and pushing the four throttles forward he pulled back on the control column and the aircraft took off heading North towards the Mediterranean and Greece.

Unknown to Hans the message from the Greeks in Athens and messages from other search stations had picked up the aircraft on its travels South and into Egypt.

At Mersa Matruh, a Middle East Air Force base to the west of Alexandria, a Beaufighter of 252 Squadron RAF took off in a cloud of desert sand and dust. Control directed the young pilot to head North West and switch on the aircraft's radar in a hope of picking off the intruder.

Some 45 minutes later a blip appeared on the fighter's radar screen and control also requested that the pilot headed to Angels Fifteen (15,000 feet) in a direction of 325*.

Hans meanwhile had switched on the autopilot (great these American aircraft –this one was even fitted with a cigar lighter, a bit like Adolf Galland's personal fighter Bf 109) and lit a small cigar. The sky was lighting in the East as they headed for Greece.

Suddenly the flight panel shattered into a mess of glass splinters as 20mm shells hosed the aircraft from stern to nose. Hans pushed the column forward and hit the right rudder pedal in an attempt to avoid the cannon gunfire. The Beaufighter flashed across the Bl7's cockpit and banked, turning back towards the bomber. Hans pulled back on the column and noticed cloud a mile or so away which could provide cover. One engine was streaming smoke but a glance across at the co-pilot revealed that his head no longer existed. Hans feathered the engine and as the next burst of cannon fire hit the rear of the aircraft the cloud enveloped the B17 and all went quiet.

Hans turned to the navigator who, although ashen faced, said that if they kept on the current course they should be in Athens in about 90 minutes.

Hopefully the RAF had given up the chase and sure enough the Greek coast appeared on the horizon. Hans dropped the undercarriage and flaps and made a rather bumpy landing back at Hellenikon.

Fact: a captured B17 operated by KG200 was intercepted while making a covert drop over Egypt and managed to get back to Athens albeit damaged.

Meanwhile back at the Oasis the two Germans were met by two officers of the Egyptian Army and were quickly taken by an army truck to the outskirts of Cairo where they transferred into a taxi and taken to a friend's apartment near the Continental Hotel.

The following day a meeting was held on a houseboat moored under the shade of a few palm trees on the Nile at Giza to the South of Cairo.

A tall slender man wearing a white suit, smoking a cigar sat at one end of the salon. Facing him was a short fat Egyptian and a taller swarthy complexioned man who had introduced himself as Al-Humidah, a Syrian from Damascus.

The tall man, one of the two Abhwer agents flown into Egypt the previous night, spoke in German and told the Syrian that it was now very likely that the German Army would never be able to return to North Africa and reach Cairo now that the Italians had surrendered and that the Wehrmacht were fighting a series of major battles against the Allies in Italy plus the fact that as the Americans were building up their military forces in England no doubt for an imminent invasion of France. These facts and that the war in Russia was proving to be very consuming on manpower and resources meant that the Middle East was no longer a priority case. However plans made earlier were still to be actioned as we still need to know of any plans by the British to move troops through Palestine and up into the Balkans.

German technical knowledge and military equipment would continue to be provided to German friendly nations. Whatever happened in Egypt, a number of individuals in the military were in place to rid the country of Farouk at the earliest opportunity and if possible initiate a guerrilla war against the British in Egypt and Palestine.

The Syrian replied by informing the German that various groups were in place throughout Syria, Lebanon and Palestine , all awaiting the day to push the British and French out and get rid of the few Jews in Palestine. However, he explained, funds were urgently needed and when were the Germans going to make the promised payments.

The German replied that the promised funds had been delivered the previous night and priority had also been given to the supply of aircraft to Turkey and that 72 of the latest FW190's had already been delivered. It was important to protect the Wehrmacht's right flank in Russia against possible attack by the Allies through Palestine and Turkey. The withdrawal of Vichy France influence from Syria and the area had not restricted military supplies to Iraq and it was necessary to keep an eye on the very fluid situation. However, he emphasised, it was important that as much intelligence that could be gathered was continued to be collected and passed to the German High Command. He continued that the reason for the meeting was to arrange for a "deep" contact that should be used to ensure that the long term plans for North Africa and Palestine be implemented

The Egyptian claimed that a South African intelligence officer had been recruited in Alexandria on his discharge from the South African army due to injuries received during the war in the desert. Apparently he was of Afrikaner stock and hated the British as some of his relatives had died in the British concentration camps during the Boer War. He was currently working for the South African government in their local consulate.

A meeting was arranged in a small bar on the outskirts of Alexandria for the following day and the Syrian left the meeting.

Fatima's Bar, Alexandria

The two Germans entered the bar and after finding their way through the dimly lit smoky interior found a table in the corner near a small stage where an overweight belly dancer was trying to convince the clientele what a beautiful woman she was.

A waiter brought two cold beers to their table and a sun tanned man approached the table with a beautiful blonde young woman on his arm. Both Germans stood and the man introduced himself as Johann Weinmann and his lady friend as Rachel Fourie. The waiter carried two more beers to the table and the conversation began about how useful the South Africans could be not only now but in the future and how funds would be paid to support their activities into Swiss bank accounts.

Agreement was reached about the gathering of intelligence and an agreement was set up so that a potential pipeline could be arranged to send any Nazis through Africa to the south of the continent and onwards to wherever.

A meeting was arranged at a local electrical store where Weinmann could pick up specialised communication equipment and details of a dead drop mailbox that had been arranged at a local hotel.

Chapter Five

London   Day Fifteen

On arriving in London I contacted Simon from a public phone kiosk in the concourse at Euston station. He confirmed that he had some information about various German groups in South America but had nothing about the Mexican connection. He said that he would e.mail me the data immediately but would like a meet as soon as possible. I suggested 11 a.m. at The Bridge House in Little Venice, Paddington, a public house situated by the Grand Union Canal.

Hailing a black taxi cab I took Rebecca to a small café in Dover Street, Mayfair, where I ordered coffees and then quickly excused myself for a few minutes, walked around the corner and entered the serviced office in Bond Street that I kept so as to pick up some fresh clothes and check for any messages. Returning to the café I noted that Rebecca was on the phone and the Italian waiter, by the look of lust on his face, had apparently fallen in love with her.

I saw that time was marching on so we left the café, hailed another taxi and told the driver to take us to The Bridge House. On arriving in Little Venice we noticed that there were a lot of blue lights flashing on various vehicles outside the pub. "Keep driving mate," I told the taxi driver and as we drove past I could see the body of a man on the pavement. The man looked like Simon, my client.

We stopped at a public house off of the Edgware Road (The Chapel in Chapel Street) and I telephoned a contact of mine at C11 (Criminal Intelligence) Scotland Yard.

"Gerry, it's Harry, I've just passed the Bridge House in Little Venice, Paddington, and it looks like it has kicked off big time there. I saw a guy lying on the pavement who I was supposed to meet so tell those who need to know and give me a bell."

Gerry promised to call me back.

A few minutes later Gerry telephoned, "Harry, a bloke called Simon has been shot as he entered the pub and the Anti-Terrorist mob are now involved. They would like to speak to you."

"Gerry, tell them I phoned Simon from a public phone box located at Euston Station at about 9.00 am and that he had requested to meet me urgently. I had suggested the Bridge House to Simon and that is all I can say mate."

I discontinued the call, turned to Rebecca; "Have your colleagues identified the man in Vienna? Also Rebecca, when were your lot told about me and my client and who told you?"

She looked at me quite angrily and replied;

"We believe that the man was an operative from BND but he fled the area after he had lost us but we are checking security cameras in the area to see if we can pick him out and identify him. "

She continued and said;

"Harry, whenever there is an investigation into neo-Nazi groups my group are automatically included in the loop and we have various sources who keep us informed."

What sources? She obviously was not going to tell me and who was she talking to on the phone at the café?

I obviously needed to consider seriously my next move as it was now apparent that there was something very serious and dangerous going on.

I checked my laptop and breathed a sigh of relief as Simon had managed to e.mail me the promised data. Yes, there were extensive details of German settlements in Argentina, Brazil, Chile and Peru but still very little about Mexico. This omission niggled me; it was like the proverbial itch that one could not scratch.

That particular lack of information decided my next move so I turned to Rebecca;

"Rebecca, have you a visa for the United States?"

She frowned but nodded indicating that she did have a current visa.

I made a couple of phone calls to Simon's bosses and some contacts in Washington DC. Later that afternoon, after shopping for a few essentials including a paperback to read on the flight, we boarded a flight from Heathrow to New York with a connecting flight from there to the Ronald Reagan Airport (a.k.a. The Washington National Airport).

I still do not know whether it was coincidence but the book I grabbed at the newsagents was "Grey Wolf", a book by Simon Dunstan and Gerrard Williams, a supposedly factual book about the escape of Hitler and Eva Braun from Germany to Argentina. During the flight to the U.S.A., before grabbing some well overdue shut-eye, I found some very interesting information about the Nazi/German settlements in South America.

Chapter Six – 1944 Berlin

Author's note: The Allies were slowly progressing Northwards up the backbone of Italy, had landed in Italy and France, the Russian Army were advancing into Poland and Germany and the Army plotters had failed to blow up Hitler at the Wolf's Lair.

The RAF and USAAF were bombing the German cities to rubble but the death camp extermination apparatus continued. Albert Speer had built armament factories underground and aircraft, tanks, artillery production increased despite heavy losses.

The wonder weapons promised by the Fuhrer were still blitzing British cities and towns but fortunately the plans to relocate the heavy water production to Germany was thwarted by the SOE using Norwegian Agents thus stopping Nazi plans to produce an atomic bomb.

In Switzerland Nazi banking officials, SS Officers and other leading Nazis were arranging the transfer of loot out of Germany.

August 1944

In Berlin a number of senior party officials attended a meeting chaired by Martin Bormann, Walter Schellenberg, Hans Lammers (Hitler's Chancellory Secretary), Dr Funk,(President of the Reichsbank) SS Brig General Spacil, and Col Pfieffer. On the unwritten agenda was the transfer of financial assets and loot stolen by the Nazis during the war and now being threatened with capture by the advancing Allies and Russians so that if the Third Reich failed a new

Fourth Reich could continue in any country that were friends of the German people thus fulfilling Hitler's destiny.

Various countries were selected but only those with large German populations were considered and South America came top of the list to be considered.

Bormann beckoned one of the SS guards at the door and whispered in the guard's ear. The guard left the room and returned with two men, an Argentinian from their Berlin Embassy and a Swiss banker. It was agreed that the two men would arrange for numbered bank accounts to be opened in Zurich for the transfer of funds from the Reichsbank. It was also agreed that where such German companies such as Mercedes had South American subsidiary companies. Transfers of funds from those companies could be made by transfers through the banking system via Switzerland to those subsidiary company bank accounts in South America. A percentage of those funds would be paid in the form of "tax" to designated Argentinian government officials and bank accounts for assistance in the possible re-settlement of those wishing to "emigrate" from Germany. The Swiss bank would, it was proposed, be paid a substantial commission for this arrangement.

Trust funds would also be set up in South American German settlements and the German subsidiary companies bank accounts in those countries would remit funds to those accounts.

The two visitors left the meeting and the only item left on the agenda was the need to arrange for a fund to pay for the disappearance of those that would be probably wanted by the conquering forces for war crimes and as these were in the main the members of the SS so it was decided that an organisation (Organisation Der Ehemaligen SS – Angeherigen or Organisation of former SS members – ODESSA) was to be set up and Schellenberg agreed to coordinate a pipeline through Europe and to the Middle East, Africa and South America.

Author's Note:: A few days after this fictional meeting a meeting was actually held on August 10 1944 at the Maison Rouge Hotel in Strasbourg where top German industrialists and bankers met to secure the future of Nazism. At this meeting was coal tycoon Kirdolf, Von Schnitzler of AG Farben , Gustav Krupp, F.Thyssen and banker Von Schroeder (a German banker who used American company ITT's German operation to fund the SS and after the war ITT were reported to be involved in political unrest in South America

Schellenberg subsequently met various SS officers and set up Die Spinne (The Spider) that organised false papers and safe houses along the escape routes out of Germany.

Meanwhile back at the Fuhrerbunker Bormann discussed the meeting with Hitler and suggested possible escape plans for the Fuhrer and Eva Braun should Berlin fall. However Hitler was adamant that he would not desert Germany but agreed to plans that would enable a Fourth Reich rise like a phoenix from the ashes if Germany fell.

At later meetings Admiral Doenitz was instructed by Bormann to ensure that three U-Boats were to be stationed at readiness at the base built in 1943 at Feurteventura in the Spanish Canary Islands within the next few months and in the meantime those boats on patrol in the Caribbean were to ship various cargoes to Mexico and Argentina prior to carrying out normal operational duties.

KG200 were advised by Max Baur, Hitler's pilot, to have dedicated aircraft (preferably captured enemy ones) available for instant use and a small airstrip was built in the Tiergarten near the Brandenburg Gate.

In Cairo the South African, Weinmann, received a coded message from Berlin instructing him to get the pipeline in place.

Berlin   April/May 1945

The city of Berlin was now a sea of rubble, Russian artillery pounded the area around the Reich Chancellery and the Reichstag, out of control fires, smoke, plus the stench of death filled air. Deserter's bodies hung from the lampposts while Russian and German soldiers fought street by street from ruined building to ruined building and the city was the nearest thing to hell on earth.

On 30 April 1945 it is claimed that Adolf Hitler and his mistress Eva Braun committed suicide in the Fuhrerbunker and that their bodies wrapped up in blankets were doused with petrol and burnt outside the bunker.

Trudi Junge, Hitler's secretary had typed his last will and testament and later claimed that she had heard the shots and saw the bodies being removed. On their deaths it had been decided that certain measures were to be taken to ensure that no trace of their identities would be found. Bormann had certainly heard of how Mussolini and his mistress had been strung up on a garage forecourt in Milan and certainly did not wish for Hitler's and Eva's corpses to become public exhibits.

Stumpfegger (Hitler's doctor) entered the room with Bormann and removed indentifying features from the two bodies some of which were placed in lined steel caskets. The remains were then wrapped in blankets and taken outside and cremated by burning with petrol.

A few hours later a small party left the bunker and at the Tiergarten airstrip a Fieseler Storch took them and luggage away from the nightmare of Berlin and headed North to Rechlin airfield.

Author's note; Based on various research by historians such as Antony Beevor; the following events took place in the Fuhrerbunker;

Magda Goebbels had poisoned her six children and with her husband, the Propaganda Minister Joseph Goebbels, committed suicide outside in the garden near the spot where Hitler and Eva Brauns bodies had been burnt and buried.

Later on the evening of May 1, the planned escape from the bunker took place an hour before General Weildling's planned surrender to the Russians at midnight. The escape party included Hitler's secretaries Trudl Junge, Gerda Christian, and Constanze Manzialy, Martin Bormann, Ludwig Stumpfegger (Hitler's doctor), SS Brigadefuhrer Mohnke, Hitler's pilot Hans Baur, bodyguard Hans Rattenhuber, Hitler Youth leader Axmann and others.

The first group led by Mohnke and including the three secretaries left through the cellars of the Reich Chancellory towards Freidrichstrasse Banhof. The other groups followed at intervals.

After the station the groups had then to cross the Spree either by the Weidendammer Bridge or a metal footbridge some 300 metres downstream. Mohnke's group chose the footbridge and headed for the Charite hospital.

The one surviving Tiger tank and a self-propelled assault gun were to be used to spearhead the escape across the Weidendammer bridge.

The word of the break-out had spread and hundreds of Wehrmacht, SS, and civilians assembled and just after midnight led by the Tiger tank rushed across the bridge. The tank smashed through the barrier at the north side of the bridge but the tank and the people following ran into heavy fire from the Ziegelstrasse and an anti-tank round hit the Tiger and many of the people following were cut down by the blast and gunfire. Reichjugendfuhrer Axmann was wounded and managed to flee, Bormann and Dr Stumpfegger although knocked over by the blast managed to continue. (Bormann was carrying the last copy of Hitler's testament)

Further attacks were made across the bridge and Bormann, Stumpfegger, Schwaegermann and Axmann continued together following the railway line to Lehrtersrasse Bahnhof at which time *they split up, Bormann and Stumpfegger heading for Stettiner Bahnhof, whereas Axmann went in a different direction but ran into a Soviet patrol. Turning back he came across two bodies who he claimed were those of Bormann and Stumpfegger (the bodies were discovered in 1972 and identified by dental records. DNA analysis of Bormann in 1999 confirmed that it was Bormann and glass fragments found in the two corpse's throat area indicated that they may have taken cyanide. However remnants of clay found on Bormann's remains were not consistent with the Berlin clay.*

The group led by Mohnke stayed together but were discovered on May 2 hiding in a cellar off the Schonhauserallee. The men were arrested but the women were allowed to go. Junge and Christian disguised themselves as men and managed to reach safety the other side of the Elbe but Manzialy became separated and it is believed that she was assaulted by Russian soldiers and like many German women at that time committed suicide but her remains have never been found.

Chapter Seven – Sweden - Feurtenventura

Those that escaped from the bunker and had boarded the aircraft that had taken off from the Tiergarten airstrip had landed at Rechlin airfield just outside Berlin. They had then boarded a DC3 aircraft that had been captured by KG200 and used for various covert operations. The aircraft took off and flew at low level so as to avoid the numerous allied and Russian aircraft still operating all over the Reich and landed at a small airstrip near the port of Keil. Some of the luggage was loaded into a truck and the passengers were taken to a local railway station from where they intended to split up and make their way to wherever.

The truck, driven by two men, dressed in workmen's overalls, headed for the harbour in the port of Keil where they found the entrance to the docks was guarded by both the German Police but being overseen by British Soldiers. The driver pulled some papers out of the glove compartment and handed them to the guard when a British Officer checked the papers out. He saw that they were shipping documents for goods from the Swedish Embassy in Berlin that were to be shipped to Gotenburg in Sweden. The truck was waved through and directed to the Swedish cargo ship "Nordic Scanda " that was moored at a berth further up the harbour.

After carefully driving around the piles of rubble and debris the results no doubt of heavy bombing by the Allies they arrived at the ship. Both men noticed the half submerged wrecks that seemed to be all over the harbour and the full impact of the destruction that this city, like so many others in Germany had suffered during this terrible war was so very apparent.

Stevedores unloaded the truck and the luggage was carefully stored in the holds of the vessel. A short time later the Nordic Scanda slipped its moorings and headed North out of Keil, Germany, heading for the Skaggerak and the Swedish port of Gotenburg.

On arrival in the port the luggage was transferred to a Spanish freighter, M.S. Emmanuel Cadiz, which immediately set sail for the Canary Islands.

Chapter Eight   Italy, Egypt. South Africa, Canary Islands

After the German surrender those Nazis that feared the hangman's noose met various colleagues in certain bars mainly in the Allied occupied zone as movement was more difficult in the Eastern Zone with the Russians challenging anything that moved. The flood of refugees throughout Europe and ensuing chaos helped cover the escape of these criminals.

Many, especially those members of the SS and Gestapo, headed down the ODESSA pipeline to Italy where false passports were issued by the Vatican in Rome and some then boarded ships in the port of Genoa that were sailing out of Europe.

Included in one of these parties was a group of men, women and children, all who had false passports obtained by ODESSA from Argentina, who boarded a rust streaked cargo ship in the port of Genoa and after a couple of days they had arrived in Alexandria. On arrival they were met by agents acting for the South African, Weinmann, and taken to safe houses in the city.

Amongst this particular group were also a number of hardened members of the SS who had been recruited in Berlin by the Muslim Brotherhood and in the following days were taken into Palestine where they linked up with various military units and helped set up training camps. The plan being to help get rid of the Jews. In other words continue Hitler's plans for extermination.

The rest, including men, women and children, were transferred down the pipeline via Khartoum, Lourenco Marques (Maputo) ending up in the Afrikaaner heartland, The Orange Free State. Amongst these families was a small dark haired child who had been orphaned, both parents dying in Berlin, and who had been adopted by a Bavarian family who had known his mother very well.

Meanwhile other Germans, including many families, left Germany and headed for South America.

Meanwhile the Spanish freighter which had taken on the special cargo from Germany at the port of Gotenburg had now recently arrived just off the Canary Islands outside the island of Feurteventura where a signalling lamp flashed across the night sky. The Ship's Master ordered the engines to be shut down and a sea anchor was dropped. A few minutes later a rubber dinghy appeared out of the darkness and a mooring rope was thrown down to the men in the dinghy.

A Kreigsmarine officer wearing the traditional U-Boat Skipper's cap climbed up the pilot's ladder and shook hands with the freighter's captain. The engines were re-started and the German piloted the freighter into a small inlet where a U-Boat lay moored.

The cargo loaded in Gotenburg was already on the deck. It was lowered onto the deck of the U-Boat.. A few hours later U-530 slipped its mooring and disappeared into the Atlantic heading South.

Chapter Nine - Day Sixteen   Washington DC

On arrival at the Washington airport, I purchased new sim cards and we fitted them into our mobiles, then as we walked through the arrivals area I noticed a man who stood amongst the waiting chauffeurs and car hire representatives holding up a sign with "Simon" my client's name clearly displayed.

Rebecca glanced at me and her face revealed that she was not too sure about this. I shrugged and walked across to the man who was quite powerfully built with a typical FBI agency haircut, white button down collar shirt and dark blue suit (and yes, like most Americans his trousers bottoms typically appeared to have had an argument with his ankles showing his white socks). I shook hands and he showed me a DEA identity card stating that his name was Joe Malone.

Joe advised that my contact, who I had telephoned earlier from London, had requested that we were to be met and that we were to be taken to accommodation that had been arranged at an unlisted address in the Arlington area.

Outside the terminal building a typical shiny black US Government Chevrolet Suburban was parked in the no stopping zone with the engine running and after we drove off, Joe said that my contact in the agency wished to meet me at their offices later that day to discuss what I required but also to update me on some recent developments.

The Suburban pulled into a residential side street in the Arlington area of Washington DC and we were ushered into a town house where Joe sorted out some take-away refreshments and told me that he would be back to pick me up at the house in three hours from now.

After Joe departed, and sitting in the kitchen picking at the pizza delivered a few minutes previously, Rebecca said, "What are you doing Harry and why are the DEA involved?"

"Rebecca the Mexican link needs exploring and if anyone know anything about Mexico, money laundering and the drug trade it's the DEA and that is why we have come to Washington. Look the financial links through Mexico that I found to these neo-Nazis really needs investigating so if I can call in a few favours with my friends here and I get a result that will be bloody good for both of us."

"That may be correct Harry but my colleagues are really not sure where your investigations were going."

"Look Rebecca I am sorry but your lot are not running me or this investigation and only I will decide what leads to follow and yes, I will accept any help that you can give me but at the end of the day – just try to observe what I do and can achieve as my aim is to get to the bottom of this funding and keep my promise to my clients in London especially Simon"

She shrugged, "OK Harry I think I'll have a long bath as the past few days have been a bit of a rollercoaster."

She disappeared in the direction of the bathroom.

45 minutes later she had still not returned and Joe was due back in half an hour. I knocked on the bathroom door but there was no answer. As the door was not locked, I knocked again and opened the door but the room was empty. Where the hell was she? I noticed that the bath was still wet and had obviously been used very recently, but the bedrooms were empty so where had she gone?

I checked the back door to the yard but that was locked and she certainly was not out there. There was no sign of her outside the front of the house either.

I telephoned my contact at the DEA and advised him of this latest development. He agreed to make some checks with various agencies and would discuss all of this when we met.

I then tried to telephone Rebecca on the phone number she had given me in Vienna but there was no answer. Bloody fool came to mind, of course there was no answer we had just changed our Sim cards and I had overlooked the need to make a note of her new number.

Joe arrived in the same Suburban a few minutes later and we left for the DEA headquarters in Army Navy Drive, Arlington very near the Pentagon. On arrival we parked in a large underground parking area where there was line after line of government vehicles mainly painted in standard U.S. Government black (somebody must have purchased a job lot and may have received a back-hander for ordering 10,000 gallons of black paint).

On passing the various security checks, that included fingerprint and optic scanning. we walked down a typical US Government office corridor with light grey painted walls, a darker grey carpet and a number of white doors to various offices but no nameplates just a discreet number on each door above the electronic door locks.

Joe placed a card into one of these locks and we entered a small office with the stars and stripes in one corner and the DEA flag in the opposite corner. On the walls were a few framed diplomas and an evocative picture of the ill- fated Twin Towers in New York before their destruction.

A short middle aged man came around from his seat behind the Government issue grey steel desk and held out his hand, "Harry you bastard , it's been too long since we last met. New York wasn't it?"

"Sammy, bloody hell it looks like you are still drinking and eating too much."

Sammy laughed; "Sit down and do not even think about lighting up one of those awful French cigarettes you inflict on everyone."

Joe left the room and we got down to business.

"Harry, after our telephone chat about your missing friend I have checked out with various contacts and a surveillance team from Homeland Security who had a 24/7 watch in place in the street where the townhouse that you used was located. They told me that they had noted a dark blue BMW parked nearby and an index check had shown that it had been rented at Washington National Airport to a German Company, the driver being listed as a F.Muller. However the Borders Agency and US Immigration have no record of any German called Muller entering the USA. In fact the German company appears to some sort of dummy set up. They had not seen anyone leaving the house except Joe after he had dropped the pair of you off earlier and then of course yourself when Joe picked you up a few minutes ago. "

"Well she cannot have just vanished into thin air but the BMW sounds a bit fishy."

"I also contacted Mossad but they have not confirmed or made any comment about Rebecca. Anyway my friend I am calling in as many favours as I can to try to find out what had happened."

We then turned the conversation to my investigation and how could the DEA help. I gave Sammy a breakdown of the background to my investigation and the need to find where this neo-Nazi funding was originating from, why suddenly Mexico had appeared as a possible conduit for these funds especially as Peru, another South American country where a few Nazis had fled to after the war because of pro-Japanese sympathies, had, it appeared, taken over from Colombia with the international drug trade. I also explained the unknown individuals who had followed me in Vienna, the unexplained murder of Simon in London and the sudden involvement with Rebecca and Mossad which I still had doubts about.

Sammy said that he was obviously aware of the Mexico still being the hub of the drug trade from South America and the Peru links but had only received scant information about any neo-Nazi involvement although he was aware of a small German settlement in Mexico which could be a good location for the transfer of drugs across the border into Texas as it was on the drug route through Central America from Peru via Mexico and then on into the States.

I asked if it was possible to gain access to the Natiional Archives & Records Administration (NA&RA) so as to check out the documents relating to the Nazi exodus to South America after the end of the war especially the transfer of assets to those countries.

Sammy picked up the phone and made a call to the appropriate contact at the NA&RA, he then nodded to me and gave me a thumbs up.

Joe came back into the room and told me that my personal things had been removed from the townhouse and were now in the vehicle outside and that the DEA were moving me to a different location. I thanked Sammy and we arranged to meet later that evening at Stetsons Bar and Grill in U.Street.

Joe took me to an apartment quite nearby in South Rolfe Street where, after a short conversation with a couple of guys sitting in a small saloon parked nearby , we entered the apartment and he told me that he would see me later and take me to Stetsons.

The fridge was well stocked and there was a secure telephone which I could use so I telephoned my client's in London at which time I updated them on the recent developments. What was quite intriguing was that no comment was forthcoming about Mossad or Rebecca. Apparently the Metropolitan Police urgently wished to interview me and anyone with me at the time about the shooting at The Bridge House.

I then rang Gerry my C11 contact at the Yard who gave me the phone number and name of the officer from the Anti-Terrorist Squad who was running the murder investigation. I immediately rang him and asked what information did he really want. He said that he wished to know what I was investigating, who I had spoken to and who was seen with me at Manchester Airport, Euston Station and later at Heathrow.

I suggested that he contacted my clients who his department knew from ongoing anti-extremist work as they could not only appraise him of my previous dealings but who would be able to put him in the picture. When I returned to the UK I would be able to, hopefully, fill in any details that he may still require.

As I replaced the receiver the telephone rang and Sammy told me that the Archives were being examined by two of his agents plus a CIA operative. Apparently the CIA wished to check these documents out because of the activities of a certain Alan Dulles of the OSS who had worked for a commercial bank in Germany before the war. He was then during the conflict working in Switzerland but negotiating with the SS and contacts in Berlin and was believed to have had some involvement in the transfer of Nazi funds to Argentina. Sammy's agents were also checking for any Nazi groups in Mexico during the war and who may still be active especially if possibly involved in the drug trade. He ended the call by saying that he looked forward to seeing me later.

I then telephoned my "banking" contact only this time using my mobile and he informed me that a detailed examination of the various fund transfers had identified a large number of individuals with German names in both South America and Mexico. He agreed to e.mail a synopsis of the names and amounts transferred as connected to them. There were also some large transfers from a Mexican company registered in Panama but background checks only identified nominee directors.

My next call was to the Weisenthal centre in Vienna and I asked to speak to "Ingrid" but the receptionist claimed that nobody of that name worked there. The plot was certainly thickening.

Joe arrived and we drove to Stetsons. The bar, a very popular establishment, was packed and the 50's jukebox throbbed away in the corner. Joe led the way through the clientele ,mainly political and government employees, where we found Sammy who had found a table away from the crowd and was sitting with a dark haired swarthy skinned man.

A pretty young waitress arrived with a tray of beer and after a quick drink Sammy turned to me and said that he would like to introduce me to Captain Jorges Duralles of the Mexican Ministerial Federal Police. Jorges shook my hand and explained that he was part of an investigation team liaising with the DEA on drug trafficking, money laundering and was very interested in potential links between Peru and any Mexican residents whatever their nationality or background.

Sammy passed me an envelope which he said contained a list of potential suspects in Mexico and front companies being used to process drug money. What they had found interesting in the intelligence that I had passed to him earlier was a bank account in a Mexican bank that was now a target for the various investigators and it was possible that there could be links to the Neo Nazis especially any residing in Mexico.

Jorges suggested that I meet him in Mexico City within the next few days and meet up with some of his team working on the Mexican drug cartels and links to Peru. This seemed a good idea and Jorges gave me his contact details, he then made his excuses and left.

Sammy had ordered some steaks and more beer. In between mouthfuls he explained that although Jorges was OK, relations between the DEA and the Mexican authorities had deteriorated recently mainly due to corruption allegations being thrown around and the Mexicans failure to close down the cartels.

He suggested that I went back to his office the following day and go through the names and organisations that his investigators had found earlier in the archives.

Chapter Ten   Day Seventeen   Off to Mexico

Joe arrived the following morning quite early and I was surprised to see Sammy sitting in the back of the Suburban. Joe told me to pack my bags as there had been some developments overnight.

Sammy handed me an envelope which he said contained the names and identities of various organisations and individuals that his guys had found in the archives. He then explained that last night the blue BMW seen earlier when Rebecca had disappeared had been found in a parking lot at the airport. Examination of CCTV recordings had revealed that the car had been parked by a young unidentified man, probably a paid delivery boy, and when the car was examined they found that it had been obviously cleaned and sanitised very thoroughly but on opening the trunk a body had been found.

I was stunned and feared the worst.

Sammy looked at me and shook his head and then gave me the name of the individual found in the trunk of the car, Jorges Duralles, our Mexican policeman. This investigation certainly was taking some very interesting twists and turns. So where the hell was Rebecca?

Sammy interrupted my thoughts;

"Look Harry there is obviously something going on that is connected to your investigations and although the relationship with the Mexican authorities are not that great at this time the murder of one of their officers so soon after meeting you, the disappearance of Rebecca from the safe house indicates some kind of conspiracy and possible leaks somewhere."

I agreed and decided that it was best to get out of town. Joe looked over his shoulder and nodded and I noted that we were heading for Andrews Air Force Base.

After passing the usual security checks at the gates we arrived beside a low hanger building where a helicopter was spooling up and ready to go. Sammy then gave me some passes and introduced me to a young guy wearing Air Force uniform and the statutory Randolph sunglasses, he then shook hands with a promise to contact me within the next 24 hours.

I climbed into the helicopter and we lifted off, the machine heading South where after some 45 minutes we landed at Stafford Municipal Airport. At the airport I managed to grab a seat on an internal flight to Atlanta from where I decided to continue South to Brazil as a visit to Mexico did not appear to be a good idea at the current time.

On arrival at Atlanta the next flight to Rio was not leaving until the following day so before I left for any hotel I purchased yet another sim card throwing the recently purchased one in Washington away. I then jumped into a courtesy car for the Marriot Hotel and booked into the place for the night. As I entered my room I decided to ring Sammy who told me that the proverbial had really hit the fan over the murder of Jorges and whereas the original suspicion was that the Mexican drug barons had contracted the murder, the blue BMW hired by a German and the strange disappearance of Rebecca or whatever her name was indicated something more. Perhaps these neo-Nazi groups that I was looking at were linked with the drug trafficking. I replied that it was a very good point and although I had decided to give Mexico a miss perhaps it may be a good idea if I checked out the German settlements in Yucatan. Sammy said he would make a few phone calls and text me a contact number of an American colleague in Cancun.

I then telephoned the airport and booked a flight on Aeromexico to Cancun cancelling the booked flight to Rio. I then contacted my clients in London. They advised that the Police still wished to speak to me about Simon's murder and that their Israeli contacts were also keen to talk to me about Rebecca. I replied that the events of the past few days really signified that there was a lot of serious activity going on and using the intelligence I had picked up I was going to follow the trail. I suggested that the Israelis leave a contact number with London so I could contact them at the earliest possible time.

I decided to get some food inside me plus some liquid refreshment so I went down to the restaurant bar area. I found a seat at the bar checking out the very large television screen mounted on the wall behind the bar staff. It was tuned into a football game and a few guys sitting down the end of the bar were obviously taking great interest in the match. There was also another man sitting alone who turned, looked at me and nodded. I thought who the hell is this? He got up and walked towards me taking the seat next to mine.

He slid a business card along the bar towards me. I glanced at it " James H Milner, D.E.A. Atlanta " He nodded to the barman and held one finger up and his glass was topped up with Jack Daniels. He then turned and held out his hand which I shook. His first words were that Sammy had called him and requested that he met me before I left Atlanta. I ordered another beer and asked as to why Sammy had requested this meet. He replied that when I go to Mexico I should stay at a hotel in Cancun as it would be a good cover as Cancun was a massive vacation resort but more importantly in the centre of the Yucutan Peninsula area of Mexico where many Germans had settled over the years. In fact they had since the time the German Army had helped the Mexicans in their many civil wars at the turn of the 19th century. He then gave me another business card with the name; Peter Colliman, Group Security Director, Hoteltur Beach Paradise, Boulevard Kukulkan, Cancun and with a direct line mobile phone number printed on it.

James explained that Colliman was of American/German stock but was employed by the DEA due to the proliferation in drug trafficking in the resort especially as many U.S. citizens vacated there and were, in some cases, good customers for the gangs. Colliman apparently had good contacts with the German community in the area and could be of great assistance to my investigations which the DEA thought could be of great importance to them. I thanked him for this information and after another couple of drinks he bid farewell and left the bar. After a good Southern style chicken meal I retired for the night and prepared for the next part of my trip.

Chapter Eleven

Kroonstadt South Africa – Argentina

The German couple with the young orphan were staying at a small farm outside Kroonstadt, a small South African Dorp in the heart of the Orange Free State. A few days after their arrival they were taken to the local railway station where, accompanied by another German family, they boarded a train which took them South to Cape Town.

At the docks, located under the shadow of Table Mountain, they boarded M.S.Chiquita, a Uruguayan registered cargo ship that was leaving South Africa for the River Plate in South America.

Meanwhile onboard the German submarine U-530 the crew were wondering what the cargo was that they had loaded in Fuertenventura. It had been locked away which obviously made them very curious.

The Captain, Otto Wermuth, announced over the vessel's speakers that, as agreed, they were heading for Argentina where there was not only a large German community but conditions for a future which would be far better than in the ruins of the Fatherland.

During the next few days, he advised that they would remain submerged as long as possible using the schnorchel during the night time hours.

The crew would also have to remain on alert as there was the risk that anti-submarine operations would continue even though Germany had surrendered.

Author's Note: Later this may have proved correct as during the night while running at shallow depth and while using the snorkel and scanning the ocean, the submarine U-530 was allegedly spotted by a Brazilian Navy cruiser Bahia, which opened fire.

However subsequent investigations by the Brazilian Navy concluded that there appears to have been an accident on the cruiser where during target practice, the ship's gun crews hit a pile of depth charges stored on the stern and the resulting explosion caused the ship to sink.

The trip weary rusty U-530 arrived off the Argentinian coast on 10 July 1945 and a dinghy took the "special cargo "to Arbwehr agents who were waiting in the dunes at Punta Mogotes. These agents had previously arrived in Argentina on the yawl Santa Barbara in July 1944.

The U.Boat then proceeded to the Argentinian Naval Base at Mar Del Plata where the Captain, officers and crew surrendered.

The M.S. Chiquita had also arrived in the River Plate and headed for the docks in Beunos Aires. The passengers disembarked and the German family were ushered through Argentinian Customs being met by a man who introduced himself as a representative of the Argentinian Foreign Ministry. Their luggage was loaded into the boot of a large

Mercedes saloon and they were then driven quickly out of the port area and taken to a military airfield on the outskirts of the city where they boarded a DC3. The aircraft immediately took off and headed South West landing several hours later at the airfield to the East of San Carlos de Barloche in the Rio Negro area of Patagonia, Argentina .

At the airfield they were met by local officials and taken to a large villa located on the edge of Lake Nahuel Huapi. The small boy commented on how the town and some of the villas reminded him of Germany as the houses were in the main built in typical Bavarian style. The scenery all around the town also reminded the family of the Bavarian Alps.

During the following days the family settled down into their new life in a place that not only reminded them of home with the snow-capped mountains nearby but the whole valley located a few kilometres out of the town seemed to be populated by Germans who had recently arrived from war torn Europe. This, together with the traditional German chalets and the local school that clearly displayed framed pictures of Hitler with swastika flags and badges on the classroom walls certainly made them feel very welcome.

A community centre had been built in the valley where each week the majority of the menfolk met and held boisterous meetings where considerable quantities of locally brewed beer was consumed along with singing the old German favourite marching songs.

Author's note::The U-530 was one of two submarines that arrived in Argentina in July 1945 some three months after the war in Europe ended. As the U-530 had taken some 5 months to sail from Europe, and the ship's logbook and crew identification documents were missing there was considerable speculation as to what its operation was really was about.

During the interrogation of the officers and crew no satisfactory answers were given as to why the voyage had taken so long and they denied carrying any passengers or prisoners of war.

What I found strange when researching for this book was the Captain, Otto Wermuth , in answer to questions, claimed that he had taken on-board one weeks' supply of fresh provisions including meat, vegetables, bread etc and 17 weeks' of special submarine foodstuffs.

He sailed from Christiansand on 3 March 1945 and admitted he was under orders from Berlin not Flemsburg (the HQ of Admiral Donitz) and his mission was to sink shipping but refused to say where.

So he took on 4 months food supplies and was at sea for nearly 5 months under the control of Berlin not Naval HQ plus his submarine had left Europe when the war had barely two months to run its course and the main Atlantic bases along the French coast were under heavy siege by the Allied Armies.

It does not appear that he was very transparent with the true reason for his mission as it evident he was on a one way trip.

Chapter Twelve

Day Eighteen   Cancun

The flight to Cancun left Atlanta early that morning and was full of happy holidaymakers heading for the Mexican sunshine, an excess of tequila and the risk of Montezuma's Revenge. I certainly needed to dress down if I was to mingle with the people staying in Cancun.

On arrival at the airport after an interminable time passing through border controls I picked up my luggage and headed for the local Hertz desk. Using an unlinked company credit card I had booked a car at Atlanta Airport and only had to present a copy the rental agreement to collect the keys of a small Chevrolet saloon. I also picked up a couple of brightly coloured t-shirts, another throw away sim card and baseball cap at one of the concourse shops.

Setting the satnav to take me to the hotel I telephoned Peter Colliman who said he would arrange a room and use a different name than my own. He confirmed that he would meet me on arrival at the hotel.

A short time later I drove past the various hotels along Boulevard Kukulkan and reached Hotel Beach Paradise. Peter, a tall blonde haired and obviously very fit guy, was sitting in the reception lobby and quickly stood up, shook hands and requested that I follow him. I followed him to the lifts and when we reached the 6th floor walked down some very well appointed corridors when we reached a door which Peter opened and ushered me in.

Peter turned, "it will be a good idea if we have a long chat so we can see if I can help you sort out this link that the DEA and you have come up with."

I agreed and we decided to have a meet later at one of the many bars along the Cancun resort. Peter then left.

Later that day I was sitting by the pool checking the backlog of messages on my laptop and glancing up now and again surveying the various beautiful women sauntering past in their skimpy bikinis (stupid place to try and work) I suddenly saw a familiar figure walking towards me.

"Shit!" It was Rebecca wearing a small white bikini that left little to the imagination I pulled a newspaper that had been left on the table up in front of my face, a recent copy of Die Mennonitissche Post (local German paper) but felt a toe pressed against my groin. Lowering the paper I looked up into her face but her eyes were hidden behind sunglasses.

"Harry" she said "why are you ignoring me?"

"Rebecca, what the fuck is going on?"

She sat down on my lounger and to be blunt it gets a bit stressful when a bikini babe sits where she did.

She leant forward and kissed my ear, whispering that we had lots to talk about.

"Rebecca, get your pretty arse up to my room in the next 30 minutes because, believe you me, we have lots to discuss."

She strutted away and I noted a phone number she had left on a scrap of tissue. On returning to my room I contacted London who gave me a contact number for the Israelis. Strange or bloody coincidence the number was the same as that left by Rebecca.

A few minutes later there was a knock on the door and a quick glimpse through the peephole showed Rebecca. I opened the door and she walked into my room. Flimsy top, tight worn denim jeans and a complete lack of make-up or perfume said it all.

I grabbed her tight and said, "What the hell is going on? You piss off in Washington, other shit hits the proverbial fan, people are dropping dead like flies. How the hell did you know I was down here so explain?"

She smiled and I felt her hand massaging below my belt. With that she dropped on her knees and unzipped my shorts. This was not going the way I intended.

She raised herself took my hand and led me through to the bedroom. "Rebecca, this is not going to answer the questions." She just smiled and undid my shorts, took off her top and pulled the jeans down over her thighs revealing a white thong and drew me close to her. In for a penny, in for a pound came to mind and for the next hour or so I had the best sex I had enjoyed for years.

She got out of the bed and walked across the room to the courtesy bar and poured two large Scotches. Then walked back to the bed and handed me one of the drinks.

"OK Harry let me explain and I must tell you I have wanted to do that since I first met you Vienna. Anyway when I went to the bathroom my colleagues rang me and said that they had identified the unknown man in Vienna. He is a member of BND but has been suspended from duty. They told me that they had discovered he had caught a flight from Frankfurt to New York and that they were extremely concerned about my safety. So I looked out of the window and saw a blue BMW parked near our townhouse but there was only one person sitting in it. Well I don't know about you Harry but if the car was being used by law enforcement agencies there would usually be two people in the vehicle not one."

"Come on love where did you disappear to, up the bloody chimney?"

She smiled, sipped some Scotch; "Near guess my friend, I hid in a wardrobe. Not very good at searching are you darling still men are never much good in bedrooms except in bed, even then most are bloody useless there as well. Seriously I knew that we were about to be picked up but figured that this guy, whoever he was would be more interested in you than me and as soon as you reported me missing I was pretty sure the locals would be on the case and any fool parked up in the area would soon be arrested."

"Fair enough but you gave me the hell of a scare especially when they found a body in the car. Until they said it was someone else I thought it was you."

"You are now making me blush."

I pulled her toward me and kissed her on the forehead holding her very tight. Damn I was getting too involved with this woman.

"Come on Rebecca, please keep me in the picture should you decide to go walkabout because this investigation is getting very dangerous. Anyway how did you know I had come down here?"

"Well after you left the house in Washington my colleagues picked me up from the house late at night leaving by the back yard and using a Pizza delivery vehicle to leave the area. We gave it a few hours and then contacted Sammy who told us that you were probably heading to Cancun and would confirm as soon as he could. So I flew straight down and it seems I arrived before you did."

We then discussed some of the recent developments and what I planned to do next.

"I know what I wish to do next Harry." She slid down on the bed and started to caress me and within seconds we were entwined and making love like a pair of lovesick teenagers.

This really getting bloody serious so I reluctantly pulled away from this beautiful woman.

"Look Rebecca I would like to spend the next hundred years making love to you but we have some work to do. Apparently near here is a long established German community and in an hour or so I will be meeting with a local DEA contact and what may then be a good idea is that as you are fluent in German plus depending on what I can find out from this contact we can drive down there acting as tourists and see what comes out of the woodwork."

"Sounds like a plan to me"

The room telephone rang and on picking up the receiver Peter said that he would meet me in the Carlos N Charlie Bar at 8 pm.

I looked at Rebecca and decided that I was not going to let her out of my sight.

"Right darling we are both off for a meet so I'm going to have a quick shower and don't worry about dressing up as we are supposed to be holidaymakers although you had better put some clothes on."

I jumped under the shower and a couple of minutes later I felt Rebecca's hands rubbing soap all over my back. I turned and kissed her and said "if you continue with this we will never get out of this room." She smiled and blew me a kiss as she covered herself in towels before going into the bedroom to get dressed.

Even without make up she looked stunning obviously the sun had given her skin a healthy glow and we left the hotel to meet Peter.

Carlos N Charlie's was not packed with holidaymakers as that apparently would happen later. Peter was sitting in a side booth and stood up as we approached his table. I introduced Rebecca and explained her participation in the investigation.

"Well Harry since we spoke I have made some enquiries and can tell you that there is an active old soldiers club in Villa Carlota, the name given to the German settlements. That may be a good place to start and I would recommend that you use a cover story of a relative who fought in the war in Europe and that you are trying to trace any relations that emigrated to Mexico."

"Yes that sounds a good idea but we will have to be careful as my German is very limited and we will have to use Rebecca as the German or Austrian relation."

"Yes sounds good Harry but don't forget how meticulous the Germans are with record keeping so there will be no room for mistakes."

"OK Peter, are you aware of any drug involvement with that community and the cartels?"

Peter shrugged; "Well most of the pushers caught here in the resort are locals, usually poorly paid employees of the cartels or dealers. In Cancun at the moment there are three main players. The first is El Diablo or that's what he calls himself, the second is an American or should I say Cuban who is linked to the mob in Florida and finally a shadow of a guy who it is rumoured to be linked to the Police."

"So there are no German connections in Cancun Peter?

"Not that I know of but you might find something up in Villa Carlota. "

"What about bank accounts do these German settlers tend to use local banks of international ones?

"Well the old timers tend to use local banks but the newer lot seem to bank with South American banks, probably because they do not trust the locals especially with all the corruption. Look Harry your best bet is to go up to Santa Elena which is more populated than the other settlement at Pustunich and have a chat with the locals."

"Yes fine but we really need a good background story. "

Rebecca said, "Look Harry there is a rumour on the street that a couple of scuba divers claim to have found some U-Boat stuff recently so perhaps we can link our visit in with that?"

"Not a bad idea. So what do you know about this Peter?"

"Well as you probably know the U-Boats were on active operations in the Caribbean during the war targeting merchant ships especially off the Florida and Texas coasts. We do know that one boat anchored off the coast near here and unloaded some crates and some of their injured crew. Perhaps that was what this scuba discovery is all about."

"OK, Rebecca get your friends at Mossad to see if we can get crew lists of the boat involved."

We then left the bar arranging to meet Peter the following day and returned to the hotel.

Back to hotel Rebecca telephoned Mossad and requested help especially any potential U-Boat links with Mexico. I ordered some food from room service and while finishing a great enchilada Rebecca's telephone rang. She listened intently and signalled me to give her some paper and a pen. The call ended and she turned to me;

"Harry this is, maybe, what we are looking for. In December 1943 a U-Boat U-530 was patrolling in the Caribbean off Martinique, Dominica and Colon and due to damage after attacking the US merchant ship Chapultepec, it is claimed that before returning back to its base at Lorient, a seaman Heinz Futter was landed in Mexico for medical reasons. Perhaps this is the guy we could claim we are related to and trying to trace?"

"How good do your guys think this information is?"

"Well they say that this particular U-Boat has quite an interesting history as after that patrol in 1943 and others during May and June 1944 it met with a Japanese submarine in mid-Atlantic where a German officer and some Japanese were transferred to the Japanese sub. Unfortunately our American friends sank the Jap submarine but U-530 escaped the ambush and proceeded to operate in the Trinidad area. But this will blow your mind as in July 1945 it appeared off the Argentine Coast where it is claimed two civilians in disguise disembarked and were landed in Argentina, people claiming it was Hitler and Eva Braun. The submarine commander, Otto Wermuth surrendered the submarine on 10 July 1945 but mysteriously the logbook and deck guns had disappeared. The US.Navy sank the submarine during a weapon testing exercise in 1947".

"Was Wermuth the skipper in 1943?"

"No that was Kapitanleutnant Kurt Lange and he commanded the sub from February 1943 until January 1945".

Author's note:: U-530 was a type 1XC/40 submarine one of only a few fitted with FumO Radar systems and was launched in 1942.

Serving with the 10th and 33rd Flotillas it served throughout the Atlantic and completed some 6 patrols. It was one of two U-Boats that arrived in Argentina in July/ August 1945 where the crews surrendered to the Argentinians.

The room telephone rang and Peter spoke;

"Harry, just picked up some information that may help you. Apparently there is a German veterans meeting held once a month at the Flycatcher Inn in Santa Elena. The next one is in two days time."

"Thanks Peter, can you book me a room there in your company's name for tomorrow night?"

"Yes no problem just let me know how you get on."

"Come on Rebecca we have got a long day on tomorrow and an early night may be a good idea."

"You don't expect to sleep do you?"

"Only after I have had my nightcap."

I was now hoping this investigation would last forever but then again I was always a bit of a dreamer.

Chapter Thirteen   Day Nineteen   Santa Elena

After breakfast of coffee and fruit we drove across the peninsula heading for Santa Elena. The Route 180 was surprisingly good being dual carriageway most of the way to Merida after which we hit a smaller road South down to Santa Elena.

During the trip we rehearsed our pretext stories so that by the time we arrived at our destination we should be able to answer any awkward questions that some bloody German may put to us.

"By the way darling we are reverting your name to Ingrid as Rebecca can be seen by some as rather Jewish, so let's not upset the bigots."

Rebecca had plaited her blonde hair in a very German style and she turned to me and asked where my leiderhosen was.

"You have got to be bloody joking Mein Frau. I prefer leather trousers on beautiful women not on some fat accordion player."

She laughed, "Mein Frau ? So I am now your wife – when did we get married," she then punched my arm and continued to flirt for the rest of the journey.

We arrived at the Flycatcher Inn later that afternoon. Pretty little place with a long verandah and plain but clean rooms. As a small Mexican woman showed us to our room I noticed an advertisement in German announcing the Veterans Meeting the following day.

Saint Elena German Military Veterans Gessellschaft

Haute Abend 20 April 2014 Geburtstagsfeier

An Kameraden Vergangenhert und Gegenwart Buffet Deutsche Weine und Bier.

20 April? Of course that was Hitler's birthday.

After dumping our bags in the room we went and sat on the veranda where the woman served us with two cold beers. Rebecca asked "Harry did you notice the collection box in the lobby?"

"Yes but it is probably better to await tomorrow's meeting to see if there were any more specific collections."

I glanced across the garden area and noticed a waste bin down the side of the main building. Always interesting what people throw away. I can still remember contracting someone to pick up some rubbish bags on the public pavement outside a private bank in Mayfair. Subsequent examination of the contents revealed details of personal bank accounts of clients including Hollywood movie stars, politicians, and other public figures.

"Rebecca, don't look now but down the side of the building is a waste container it will be a good idea that before we go if we get the opportunity we have a look at what may be discarded by the people attending this celebration tomorrow. If anyone asks what we are doing we just tell them you lost something in the room and think that you may have thrown it away by mistake."

A grey haired gentleman wearing a panama hat, light coloured cotton jacket and dark slacks walked onto the verandah.

He sat at the adjoining table and the little woman came out carrying a tray with a glass and a bottle of German beer.

I ordered two more beers and the woman returned with two local brews. I nodded to the stranger;

"That looks better than this stuff." (raising my glass in a toast).

He smiled; "Guten Tag, you are British?"

"Yes but my wife Ingrid is Austrian"

"So on vacation?"

"Yes and No; we are trying to trace any relatives of a German sailor who did not return from a U-Boat patrol in the Gulf of Mexico in 1943. He is a distant cousin of Ingrid."

"Some here may be able to help you. We are having a meeting tomorrow perhaps you would like to come. I am sure the association secretary will be able find whether your long lost cousin was here in Mexico."

"That would be terrific wouldn't it be darling?"

"Ja, I would welcome the opportunity to find out what happened to Heinz."

The old man raised his eyebrow; "Heinz? I knew a Heinz, it would be good to talk tomorrow." With that he finished his beer and left.

After a snack we retired for the night and agreed that things were getting very interesting. I telephoned Sammy who said that nothing new had been received but the Mexicans were getting a bit pissed off with the lack of progress in respect of the murder. They had also heard about some Limey Bastard and had asked who the hell he was.

Rebecca phoned her Mossad friends and they advised that the German traced to Washington had now gone missing.

Day Twenty   Veterans Meeting

The following day after breakfast we took a short stroll through the settlement. It certainly did not look very German the small single storey houses tending to be very plain and simple. However there were a number of German surnames on the mail boxes.

"Come on Rebecca let's get back to the hotel, I've got an idea."

In the lobby I had seen a local telephone directory so grabbing it I ushered Rebecca into our room.

"Here are the target names that I have come up with so far, let's see if we can find any matches in this directory."

We spent the next few hours cross checking the names and found two matches. Of course these two could be just people with the same surname but it would be interesting if these two were at the Veterans celebration. One of the names we also noted in the directory struck me as a bit of a coincidence "Futter"

"Shit- isn't that the name of the long lost relation? We really need to get a bit of family background on this guy, you know names of uncles, aunts, brothers, sisters, even the bloody dog's name. If this guy is still alive and at this celebration and he or his relatives start asking questions we could be proverbially stuffed"

Rebecca picked up her phone; "Damn Harry, I cannot get a signal, can you?"

My phone was also showing no signal so it looked like we were going to have to wing it.

Rebecca picked up the phone in the room but I told her that making a call to her colleagues by using the public line could be risky.

As there was no Wi-Fi either at the hotel we were incommunicado so to speak.

At 11 am we both entered the small bar area where a few of the veterans had already arrived. In the background a CD player was pumping out German oompah music and two women dressed in Bavarian costume with low cut blouses were serving steins of frothy beer. I accepted one but Rebecca chose a large glass of Hock.

The old gentleman seen earlier walked across the room and greeted us, signalling to a lean elderly guy standing at the end of the buffet table. He walked towards us carrying a collection box and on our introduction bowed and said;

"Perhaps you would like to make a donation to our social fund"

"Yes, of course but is the same fund as in the collection box in the lobby?"

"Nein, this is a fund dedicated to those who have served, the other box is for the families who have lost loved ones over the years."

"Can I make a card payment?"

"Ja, we can use the machine at the end of the bar." He turned and collected the machine, an old roller swipe card type and he produced a payment slip which I completed donating a $100 to the cause being careful to use a company credit card whose origins would be difficult to trace.

"Danke – you are very generous, now I understand you are trying to trace a German seaman who may or may not have arrived in Mexico during the war?"

Rebecca spoke; "yes he was a second cousin removed of my mother's side of the family who lived as far as we know in a small village in the Tyrol."

"What was his name this seaman related to your family?"

"Heinz Futter, we believe that he was he was a crewman on U.530."

"Oh yes, the submarine that ended up in Argentina. Otto Wermuth was the Captain I believe."

"No, when he went missing just before Christmas in 1943, the Captain then was Kapitanleutnant Kurt Lange I believe."

"I believe you are correct Frau but I do not think a relation of yours came here."

"Are you sure?"

"Yes positive, look Heinz here knows everyone in the settlements and being a Kriegsmarine veteran who did indeed serve in the U.Boats during the war would certainly know whether any sailor arrived here who came from the Tyrol. Isn't that right Heinz?"

The old gentleman nodded and said, "I never introduced myself, Heinz Futter at your service. Yes I did serve in the Kriegsmarine but have never been near or to the Tyrol in my life and I certainly have no family there. What relations I did have died in the bombing of Hamburg during the firestorm in 1943. It would appear that you have possibly got your facts wrong. I am sorry if you have had a wasted journey. It may be a good idea if you get in touch with the Kreigsmarine Archive in Keil. They may be able to give you better information."

The guy with the collection box interrupted;" Our special guest speaker has just arrived so we will have to finish this conversation. If you wish to stay you are welcome although all the speeches will be in German so you may get bored."

I looked at Rebecca and said, "you are probably right Herr Futter, we will leave you to your celebrations and we hope all goes well."

We bid farewell and left the room.

Back in our room I told her to pack our bags.

"I think they sussed us and I think I have got what I came here for."

"Really Harry, what have you got?"

"Details of two bank accounts the one where I made the donation is the same as the one where large sums are going in and out of it. The other account appears to be with a local small Mexican bank but it will be interesting to check out any connections."

"That's great but who do you think the speaker was tonight?"

"According to the reservations register it is a guy with the surname Wolffe. Would be interesting to check him out so once we get out of this place we can contact the outside world. Come on darling let's leave as I think we have outstayed our welcome."

We left the keys in the room door and drove off back towards Cancun.

As soon as we could get a decent phone signal Rebecca telephoned Mossad, putting the phone on speaker mode, she updated them in respect of the situation found back at the Inn.

"Thanks Rebecca, we have been trying to contact you as we have some important updates for the pair of you."

"Yes sorry we had no signal and the security of the landline at the Inn could have been extremely doubtful."

"Well the news is that Futter was not in the Kreigsmarine but was landed in Mexico as an Arbwehr agent and the events in Europe stopped his return home. The other news is that the

German who has been following you has obtained photographs of the pair of you and he has got a team of gophers running around Cancun trying to locate you guys."

"How the hell did he get the photos?"

"Well the one of you Rachel looks like it comes from a cctv recording from a security camera outside the Simon Westhanfall centre in Vienna, whereas Harry's was, it appears, taken while he was sitting outside a café in London."

I interrupted , "That changes things so we will not be heading back to Cancun as planned so we will update you once we decide our next move. While you are at it can you check out a retired German Officer called Wolffe?"

"Yes fine, good luck you guys and be careful."

Rachel turned to me; "this is getting more serious every day so what are we going to do next?"

"At the moment I am thinking about that bloody Red Volkswagen Beetle that has been sitting on our arse for the last 10 miles as every time I slow down they do and when I speed up they accelerate. Don't turn round just have a look in the mirror in the sun shield."

"We are going to have to lose these guys Harry because they are probably making phone calls with a running commentary right now."

"Check the map in the glove box and see if there is a filling station coming up."

"Yes in about 8 miles on our side of the dual carriageway"

"Any turn offs before or after the filling station that will let a car turn back to the site if the driver misses the entrance?"

"No Harry, nothing whatsoever."

"Good tighten your seatbelt and hang on darling."

I accelerated and the speedometer needle crept up and we were soon hurtling along at 90 mph and I just hoped we would not fall foul of the Mexican Highway Patrols. The Volkswagen followed and managed to keep pace so I gradually decelerated so they were closer to our rear fender than before.

Soon the Pemex filling station signs appeared in the distance so I accelerated and the Volkswagen moved closer.

As we approached the forecourt entrance I accelerated and right at the last second swung the car to the right onto the forecourt. The driver of the VW was taken by surprise and missed the entrance and despite braking furiously with blue smoke emerging from the car's locked wheels the driver was forced to continue on the carriageway as a large truck was fast approaching and bearing down on his car from behind.

Fortunately there were few vehicles on the forecourt and we skidded to a halt near the sales kiosk. What interested me was a public service coach refuelling at one of the diesel pumps.

"Quick Rebecca, grab your things. We're going on a bus ride."

I locked the car and on establishing that the bus was going to Cancun we climbed on the bus and found seats at the rear amongst what appeared to be a number of locals mainly old men, women and a few children.

The bus moved off out of the filling station and headed East towards Cancun. As we passed a parking area I nudged Rebecca and pointed towards the VW that was parked on the side of the highway. Two men could be seen sitting inside, obviously waiting for us to pass by. They were in for a long wait.

I telephoned Peter and asked him to meet us at Cancun and would advise him where we were getting off the bus preferably not at the bus station or in the centre of town..

I also telephoned Sammy and suggested that we meet as soon as possible within the next few days but preferably very covertly as it appeared that not only had there been leaks but other serious players in the equation. He agreed and promised to get back to me within the next hour.

The bus was now approaching the outskirts of Cancun and I told Rebecca that we should get off before we reached the town centre.

I noted some small shops on the side of the highway so rang the bell requesting the driver to stop. The bus pulled up outside Rancho El Milangro, a bar/restaurant on the Cancun Valladolia. We entered the bar and ordered some coffee then I telephoned Peter and requested that he sent someone to pick us up and take us to the airport but do not come himself as I was pretty sure that he may be under surveillance. He agreed and said that someone would be with us within the hour.

My phone then rang and Sammy said that he had arranged a flight down to Belize City and the aircraft would pick us up at Cancun Airport but we had to go to an airfreight company located just outside the airport perimeter. He would advise the time and date but it would probably be early tomorrow.

"It looks like we have got to find somewhere to stay tonight Rebecca. Still not a bad idea as we can sort out some of these links and bank accounts plus I can get my experts to do a bit more tracing."

"Fine I feel the need to have a short bit of rest and relaxation as the last few days in bed with you, being chased by mad Germans have been like a whirlwind and, my God, sometimes I wonder where the hell I am and what day of the week it is."

"You are bloody lucky. I can think of loads of women that would love to be in your place.*

She punched my arm; "Arrogant bastard comes to mind but yes I must say I do enjoy your company especially at night."

I leant across and kissed her.

The barkeeper said they had accommodation in a villa at the rear of the restaurant so, paying him a few pesos, he gave me the keys to the place.

I phoned Peter, told him to cancel the driver and told him I would be in touch. Rebecca telephoned her colleagues and gave them an update while I discovered that there was a computer internet link at the bar and sent some e.mails to my client and my banking specialist laundering the messages through covert links.

As it was now early evening we decided to order some food and then get some shuteye. The barman also arranged for a local taxi driver to pick us up in the morning.

Authors Note: It's strange on writing these notes while relating this story that how the majority of the world perceive what Mexican food basically consists of such as Chilli Con Carne (a Texas invented dish) Enchilladas, Tacos, Burritas etc whereas there is a lot more to Mexican cuisine.

We ordered a meal that represented the region (Yucatan was the centre of the Mayan world as many tourists have discovered with the various temples and ruins that can be seen near Cancun) so a starter of Minilla De Pescado , followed by Tamales Verdes de Pollo went down a treat especially washed down with cold Gruet Brut Rose, a long established Mexican wine.

We finished with a couple of shots of Tequila and headed for the villa.

Checking my e.mails and intelligence collected to date I could see that the Mexican bank account set up for "donations" was being "smurfed" (this means that cash is being paid into the account in many transactions all being under the reportable limit in respect of any anti-money laundering regulations. So unless some clerk was checking these statistics to add up the total banked on any particular day the bank would not pick this up. The other equation or cash flow analysis showed that there was some kind of imbalance in that I could see donations coming in but many appeared to have been deposited from various bureau de changes in areas where I had no intelligence in respect of German settlements or Neo-Nazi activity. Also funds were going out of the account to organisations that appeared to have nothing to do with veterans groups.

I e.mailed my banking contact and asked him to urgently check out these recipients.

Rebecca had now started to undress – damn I was now being completely distracted. "Come on darling – give me a break." She walked across the room wearing nothing but a small pair of panties.

"Harry, relax for God's sake, unwind or you will have a heart attack,"

I poured myself a large Scotch and walked towards her.

"Listen to me darling, it has been a long time since I had such feelings but you are now really getting to me."

She just smiled grabbed the waistband of my trousers and kissed me very, very passionately.

All I can say that the bed was big, the woman was stunning and the night was too short.

I awoke some hours later feeling her mouth exploring my body.

I grabbed her and the following moments had me exorcising my emotions of the past few days with her shouting and digging her fingernails into my buttocks.

No pain, no gain came to mind.

Chapter Fourteen   Day Twenty One   Belize

The following morning there was a knock at the door, the taxi had arrived and we headed for the airport.

Rebecca was purring like a cat with her pretty head on my shoulder while en-route to the airport. (This shit was getting pretty serious).

We arrived at the freight office (Air America crossed my mind, the CIA operation in South East Asia), I gave the keys of the hire car I had dumped to the receptionist and a guy walked us out to an aircraft out on the tarmac.

A USAF C130 Hercules stood on the tarmac with all engines running. On climbing aboard we were directed to seats down the side of the cargo bay.

"Hello Harry."

Sammy sat opposite.

"Hello my friend, you have not met Rebecca have you? Anyway here she is and we really have lots to talk about."

"Yes we do. Hello Rebecca, my God, I now understand why this bastard sitting next to you has his arm around you. Take care he is dangerous.

When we last spoke Harry we had the crap about a leak, we now appear to have some mad man looking for you guys, and we now really wish to know what the fuck is going on."

"Sammy we will talk about that at our meeting but it appears that the leaks are either with Mossad or your mates at the DEA, but seriously my friend I suspect the CIA."

"Fuck"

"Yes, that about sums it up"

The flight was quite short and the aircraft started to descend and we were soon landing at the airport in Belize.

A U.S. Consulate Chevrolet met us on a hard standing on the opposite side of the airport to the terminal buildings and we drove into the city arriving at the Princess Hotel & Casino.

Sammy had booked a conference room through the Consulate and refreshments were laid out on a buffet table. Collecting coffees we sat down around the conference table I then began to update Sammy.

"Right my friend the German Veterans in Mexico have two bank accounts both being registered as Charities, one appears to be very much a local account used for paying for meetings and printing of brochures and that kind of thing. The second is very important as it is in the branch of a Cayman Island bank and funds are transferred to the Caymans through a Mexican Bank in Mexico City. Now that account is bloody interesting as when you go through the entries there are donations not just from the Germans in the Yucatan but from what looks like other German groups in Canada, California, Peru, Brazil and Argentina.

This account appears to be a hub account with most of the donations being transferred on to accounts set up in various company names most of which are registered in Panama with nominee directors.

I suspect that the donations which are made to these charities are in fact monies from the sale of narcotics and for the privilege of using these accounts to launder the cash the Germans get a nice cut and that cut ends up in the Caymans."

"Jesus, Harry that is one hell of an idea but how can you prove it?"

"Well if you analyse the bank statements you will see that the so called donations are disproportionate to the number of members in each of these Veterans groups or the lot of them are multi-millionaires. One of the Panama companies is known to be behind a Cash & Carry operation in Miami which is also a good way to launder money."

"OK, we can certainly work on that but why is this German nutter chasing you half way around the world?"

Rebecca spoke; "The man is with BND the German Secret Service but is currently suspended because of suspected corruption. Apparently he was being paid by the Muslim Brotherhood to infiltrate various anti-terrorist operations across Europe. A Palestinian prisoner spilt the beans having met this man while he visited Damascus. It was not until Harry spotted him in Vienna that we had any idea what he looked like."

"But what is this about the leaks Harry."

"Christ Sammy the whole investigation has leaked like a bloody sieve. I have been under surveillance from the minute I met my client in London. Then I was followed around Vienna, someone knew about me meeting with Simon who was then gunned down in Paddington, then someone knew of the first safe house in Washington and staked it out, the murder of the Mexican cop and then the photos of us circulated around Cancun. Plus of course yesterday we had the bloody Krauts chasing us down the highway."

"Well, have you any ideas Harry?"

"Could be anything from phone tapping, computer hacking, a team of operatives watching the main characters and I say that because I telephoned Simon that day he was murdered from a public phone box on Euston Station directly to his mobile and I suggested the meet location so unless someone hacked his mobile he must have been followed from his office to Paddington.

The other link is the CIA one and I say that because they seemed rather keen to go with your guys to check out the archives. Now I think that was probably due to the Dulles involvement with the Nazis during the war when he was with the OSS in Switzerland or the bastards have some black operation going on."

Rebecca's phone rang; and I watched her grab a pen and make a few notes. The call ended and she turned to us;

"That guest speaker Wolffe – well he has a very interesting background; SS officer in Athens, Belgrade and Rome. On a list of wanted War criminals but last seen in Genoa in 1945. The other information is that someone broke into your room Harry at the Cancun Hotel they obviously did not know we had gone."

"What are your plans now Harry?"

"Well there is still an imbalance between funds going to that hub account especially those originating from South America and only some of those I suspect are drug monies. If you can get your forensic accountants to sort out these bank accounts Sammy I think you will be able to confirm that these accounts are being smurfed and being charity bank accounts none of the bank's compliance people appear to really have had a close and proper look as to what is going on."

"Smurfs darling?"

"Yes it's a term for people, usually gophers, going into branches of say a certain bank with cash but below the amount that has to be reported under money laundering controls. So say in one day you might have fifty deposits all ending up in the same bank account that may total fifty times more than the reportable limit."

"OK Harry so we'll analyse the accounts and check out our guys in Panama to see if we can establish the real beneficiaries of these funny companies. Oh yes Rebecca have your guys got a name for this rogue German?"

"Yes, they just texted it to me when they called about Wolffe, his name is Werner Bruin and he was originally with the Stasi prior to the unification of Germany so he was probably trained by the KGB."

"Can your guys get me a photo of the bastard and tell them to give me a call as soon as possible."

Rebecca picked up her phone and asked for the photograph that Sammy had requested then handed the phone to Sammy.

"Hi there,we have spoken before and you have my secure contact details in Washington so can you send the picture there but I would like to ask you to do me a big favour. Circulate his details to both Scotland Yard and to the Head of the Drug Squad in the Mexican Police as the bastard is as far as I know still in Mexico and tell them he is suspected of murdering one of their officers a few days ago in Washington DC. The Brits will probably be able to tie him in with the murder in London as well."

He handed the phone back to Rebecca who, after a few words, she ended the call.

"Yes Sammy they are going to contact the Mexicans and Brits and you should have the photographs in your office within a few days."

"Right Harry where are you off to now?"

"Peru seems a good idea because not only are there quite a few Germans living there but they as you know appear to have taken over from the Colombians with the export of drugs."

"Well my friend that is one hell of a trip you are on but I can certainly put you in touch with our people down there but I think your flight schedule could be a bit chaotic as not much flies in that direction from this dump."

Rebecca switched on her laptop and after a few minutes she clapped her hands; "Sammy you are full of shit, United and Avianca fly to Lima from Belize Airport, I'll book a couple of tickets there is a flight leaving at 5.20pm today."

"Hang on love we had better not use our real names just in case some nosey sod is scanning the airline flight passenger manifests and tells the wrong bastards."

"I thought this would happen so let me book the flights as though they are for two diplomats travelling for Uncle Sam."

"Thanks Sammy and let me know what it costs and don't forget I will need some contact details in Lima."

Sammy then booked the tickets and suggested we had lunch sent up before we made our way to the airport.

We were taken to the Philip S W Goldson International airport and entered the small departure lounge and found a couple of seats in Jets Bar, I wondered why they had chosen such an original name, probably me just being sarcastic.

However we were soon on our way to Lima scheduled to arrive there early the following morning.

Chapter Fifteen   Day Twenty Two/Three   Lima, Peru

On arrival at Jorge Chavez International Airport and after the usual security measure of new sim cards, I grabbed a hotel courtesy car which took us to the Ramada Costa Del Sol a short distance from the airport.

"Right darling I am going to phone Sammy's man and see what he can tell us about any known links between the drug syndicates and any German locals. Perhaps you can get some local intelligence from your guys as I understand many of the Germans who came here were of the Jewish faith. Then I am going to have a long, long bath with you."

She walked towards me, smiled and said that she would enjoy that.

Sammy's contact agreed to meet at lunchtime and would send a car to pick us up. Rebecca in the meantime had spoken to Mossad and they told her about a German settlement in central Peru named as Oxapampa but the city had been settled by Prussians and Tyroleans in the 19th century well before the Second World War.

However a couple of years ago a local Peruvian of native descent, Martin Quispemayta had formed a movement APNM (Andean Peru National Socialism Movement) and he was trying to get the Government to rid the country of its 3000 Jewish citizens. Apparently press reports at the time had revealed that when he was interviewed by the media he was yet another Holocaust denial merchant and even went as far as claiming the Spanish Conquistadors who had invaded Peru all those centuries ago were all Jewish. He sounded a real nutcase but possibly a dangerous one so who were funding this idiot?

Editor's Note: Fact as reported in the Jewish Chronicle on 21 August 2012.

"Might be a good idea Rebecca if you try to join the movement and get a list of members as you can come across as a dedicated Nazi whose grandparents were killed during the war."

"Could be risky so let's see what the local DEA man knows."

However on making a quick search on the internet revealed that there was no sign of the group just a couple of reports about the various newspaper interviews a couple of years ago.

The search also showed that the Headquarters of the APNM had been located on the Avenida Alfonso Ugarte in Lima with photographs of Quipemayta dressed in a brown shirt with a similar looking red, white and black armband standing on a balcony (a bit like those old photographs of Adolf all those years ago) but a Google earth search at street level along the Avenida could not identify whether the headquarters were still there unless all the signs have been taken down since the media articles were published.

"Come on Harry lets have that bath but this investigation into this group certainly has possibilities."

After a very enjoyable soak with a beautiful woman (funny what soap does in certain places) my telephone rang and Sammy advised that the local DEA guy was sitting outside the hotel in a dark blue Mercedes with a hubcap missing from the nearside front wheel.

We made our way down to the hotel car park and quickly found the Mercedes where the driver introduced himself as Frank Mitchell, showing his DEA identification card, and we drove off towards the centre of town. Frank explained that we were heading for a place called Bar Maury which. although it was a bit of a tourist attraction, we could easily mingle with the tourists and discuss things without being noticed by any prying eyes. We soon arrived at the bar, an old established place in the historical centre of Lima. Although there were many customers in the premises taking "selfies" with their mobile phones and creating a hubbub of background noise we soon found a table in the beautiful wood panelled bar.

Frank ordered some drinks and we got down to business. He did not know of any involvement of any Germans with the Peruvian drug cartels but knew a little about the APNM which was run by individuals descended from the Incas who were seen as second class citizens by the white minority. What about their funding did he know who paid for their premises, publications and their operation?

Frank did not know but he said that he suspected it came from outside of Peru possibly Chile or Argentina as there had been a large number of Nazis settling in those countries after the war.

I told Frank that my initial investigations had not revealed any bank account in the name of APNM did he have any ideas where they kept their money. Frank laughed and told me that I was dealing with an organisation that was basically run by Peruvian peasants and their money was probably kept in a suitcase under the bed. Anyway he gave me a list of known members of the organisation which may help me with my investigation.

It certainly did not look as though there was any benefit going out to the German settlements but a check out of the APNM headquarters may be an option as we may find another piece of the jigsaw.

Frank was not sure if they were still at the Avenida Alfonso Ugarte but suggested we drive down there to see if anything was going on. He warned us to be very careful as there was an inherent distrust of white people, especially foreigners in the area and that is why he had brought us to this bar as we had mingled easily with the clientele who had probably assumed that like them we were just tourists.

We finished our drinks and left the bar, Frank driving us to the building where the APNM headquarters had been located. When we arrived I left Frank and Rebecca in the car which Frank had parked in a side street and walked towards the building last reported as being the HQ of this neo-Nazi organisation. The balcony was still there but the building appeared to be empty with the windows being boarded up although the entrance door was open.

I quickly entered the hallway and it became immediately apparent that the place had been unoccupied for some time and except for some litter and discarded rubbish on the floors there was no evidence of the APNM ever being there. As I was leaving the building I noticed a small collection box laying in the corner of the hall. A quick examination showed that it was empty except for a bank deposit slip. Bingo it was to the APNM's bank account. I quickly returned to the car and Frank drove us back to our hotel.

Before he departed Frank advised us to keep a low profile as like most Latin American countries corruption in Peru was widespread and the drug syndicates were very powerful with lots of influence.

I telephoned my banking specialists to get an urgent breakdown of the bank account then spoke to my clients to give them an update of what was going on. When asked about APNM they told me that they had known about the group but understood that it had closed down and that is why Simon had not told me about them when I started the investigation.

A few hours later I received an e.mail from my financial specialist which showed that the APNM account had been closed but previous transactions identified transfers of funds from the Mexican hub bank previously identified plus some cash transfers from a Colonia Dignidad in Chile.

Rebecca said; "I know of that place it was set up by an ex SS guy Walter Ruaff I believe. It was operating as a cult with tortures, child abuse, very strict rules and so on. I think the Chile government prosecuted a few Germans running the place and then closed it down as a cult."

"Sounds like a South American Holiday camp."

"Yes I believe the place had barbed wire fences and watch towers and don't forget quite a few Nazis fled there at the end of the war and there were rumours that Mengele worked there for a while experimenting with chemical weapons. Yes I now remember a bit more about the place, I think it changed its name to Villa Baviera and was run by another Nazi, Paul Scafer who ended up in prison where he snuffed it."

I telephoned Sammy and asked him what he knew about this Chilean holiday camp.

"Harry, that is the place used by Pinochet and his thugs to carry out experiments of political prisoners. You will never guess who were involved with that place."

"Who ?"

"Our secretive friends across the park the CIA"

"You have got to be bloody joking."

"No Harry, do you remember a certain Michael Townley, the CIA assassin? Well he, it is claimed, carried out assassinations all over the world and some of these murders included allegedly, the Swedish Prime Minister, and some on behalf of Pinochet. The bastard even worked down in Chile at Villa Baviera where he helped the local chemists develop chemical weapons when he was not arranging the death of whoever."

Fact- Townley is indeed in a Witness Protection Program after being arrested in connection with an assassination attempt in Washington DC."

"Where is he now?"

"Witness protection programme but it is a possibility that while operating in Europe he and his colleagues could have bumped into our German friend, Herr Bruin."

"Sammy, the bits seem to be fitting together all we need now is to tie up the Argentina and possible Chile connection and then see if the Cayman Islands are the Americas financial link between the European neo Nazi groups especially if it is related to the international drug trade. So I think we will go South and see what we can find. By the way have you any news about our German friend?"

"Well Peter rang from Cancun and the CCTV captured the bastard boarding a flight heading for Beunos Aires. He was travelling under the name Vendermann but it is possible on arrival he may use a different identity. So keep your eyes peeled."

"Thanks Sammy, speak to you soon my friend."

I then checked the flight schedules to Chile and to check out whether there were any flights to a town near Villa Baviera. Yes LAN airlines operated to Concepcion on the Chilean coast and I could see that there was an airstrip at Villa Baviera. Rebecca said that the camp had opened its doors to tourists so we may be able to stay there. I booked a flight using Rebecca's Travel Company credit card which was leaving Lima the following morning. I then asked the concierge whether there was anywhere local that could print us some laminated business cards with our photographs on. He said there was such a place at the airport and they usually printed the cards while you waited.

I then asked Rebecca for the card that she had shown me all those days ago in Vienna.

"If I rang that telephone number and asked for you would they confirm that you worked there at Exodus and was a travel agent?"

"Of course, why do you ask?"

"Well darling give them a call and ask them to add my name to their employee list because I think someone may be calling them within the next few days."

Rebecca rang the number and speaking in Yiddish I heard her spell out my name.

When she finished the call she then rang the hotel at Villa Baveira and booked a room in our names explaining to whoever answered the call that we were employees of Exodus, a European Travel Agency and that we were researching new and unique hotels in Latin America. She also asked what the transport links were between the hotel and Concepcion. She ended the call and turned to me;

"Yes we have a room and the best way to the hotel is by air and a small aircraft flies there from the airport at Concepcion on a mail run and they also take passengers. The plane lands at the airstrip built when the camp opened years ago otherwise it's a long bus trip to Parrall which is 35 kilometres from the hotel."

I telephoned the airline flying us down to Chile to check the availability of the flights from Concepcion to Villa Baviera and they confirmed that a flight was leaving a couple of hours after we landed. So they booked us both on it.

Rebecca then received an e.mail from her "travel agency" who confirmed that they had received a telephone call from the hotel at Villa Baviera, the caller requesting the agencies address as the hotel wished to send some publicity brochures and whether either of us had mobile phone numbers in the event the hotel needed to contact us. They had been told that the company telephones we used were only used in

Europe and while in the Americas the staff tended to use different sim cards so as to keep down costs and use cheap pay as you go phones. However the caller had been given the address of a serviced office in Vienna.

I wondered who Herr Braun was meeting in Argentina and there was no doubt he was going to warn whoever about my investigation. As an international arrest warrant had been circulated by the FBI, Mexican Authorities and Scotland Yard he was going to have to be bloody careful.

Early the next day we left the hotel for the airport where I quickly located the print shop and showing them Rebecca's card asked them print off a few cards in our names, put our photographs on them and laminate the cards The assistant said they would be ready in half an hour and suggested that we go and have a coffee while we waited.

We had no sooner sat down in the café when two men approached the table and sat down opposite us. The older of the two pulled an identification card out of his jacket pocket and a leather wallet which I could see contained an official looking badge.

He introduced himself and his colleague and stated that they were officers in the Peruvian Technical Police. He then asked what I was doing snooping around the building on Avenida Alfonso Ugarte yesterday.

I told him that I had been asked to see if the previous residents were still active and operating from there by a business contact in England. As it was apparent that they were long gone as far as I was concerned that was the end of the matter. He replied that it probably was but we in Peru do not like strangers entering private premises without appropriate authority. I apologised and he said that this time he would accept my apology and asked where I was going to next. I replied Chile to check out some hotels and finish the rest of my honeymoon. He smiled, congratulated me while checking Rebecca out and stood up to go. His final words were to be careful in Chile as the authorities there can be far more dangerous than us.

We collected the cards and boarded the flight to Chile.

Chapter Sixteen   Patagonia/Egypt

The Nazis living in the valley ensured that they were self sufficient growing most of the vegetables needed and buying other essentials from San Carlos de Bariloche and San Martin de los Andes. Locally the valley was known by the Germans as the Centre and consisted of three small neighbourhoods

Ex SS Officers initially controlled the Centre and the family with the small boy, now identified as Albert Brunger, moved into a mansion named Inalco located on the Inalco Estate where there were also a number of underground bunker chambers and for security only one way in and out of the place. The boy's education was by private German tutors at the house.

In the following years some of the residents became bored and some individuals such as Eichmann moved to the big cities such as Beunos Aires. Of course Eichmann, who subsequently worked as a foreman at the Mercedes Benz factory in that city, was traced by Mossad agents, kidnapped by them in 1960 and taken to Israel to face trial and subsequent execution.

Mengele "The Angel of Death" left San Carlos de Bariloche, where he had apparently worked as an illegal abortionist, when he heard of Eichmann's kidnap, fleeing to Paraguay and then to Brazil where he suffered a heart attack while swimming and died in 1979.

Gold, cash and other loot stolen by the Nazis some being shipped to Argentina by U-Boat during the war had been laundered by the Perons and invested in a number of multi-national companies. It is believed that when the Peron's fell from grace large sums of money and assets were transferred out of Argentina into Brazil.

However back at the Centre in Patagonia the German community continued with their way of life. Some of the war criminals of course were discovered and extradited for various war crimes back to face justice in Europe.

Albert continued his education and in 1960, after visiting Beunos Aires, where he obtained a West German Passport, he flew by Aerolinas Argentinas to Geneva where he attended Universite de Geneve studying art and design.

On 23 August 1962 Albert visited a private bank located in downtown Zurich where at a meeting with a German member of Odessa and a director of the bank discussed the transfer of funds to an account in South America. As the political scenario in Argentina was, with the demise of the Perons, somewhat fragile it was agreed to place the funds into a Brazilian account. The massive funds paid to the Perons by Bormann were discussed and the Odessa member produced an affidavit signed by Bormann and Hitler that agreed to the transfer of what was left after the Argentinians spending spree to another account in the Brazilian banking system less certain administrative payments to the bank.

On departing from the bank Albert decided to visit a coffee bar in the town centre where he was served by a young Swiss waitress, Inga Rafalle. The meeting developed into a relationship and in 1964 the couple married with a baby boy Frederick being born in April 1966.

Albert returned to Patagonia with his young family and continued his residence in the Inalco mansion. The boy started his education at the school in San Carlos de Bariloche and his father Albert took over the management of the Centre. A few of the original residents had, by this time, travelled the short distance to Chile and set up Colonia Digitas which later was re=named Villa Baviera.

In 2005 Albert died and his son, Frederick, inherited his father's estate.

In the Middle East the continuing war against the State of Israel had been an ongoing problem since 1948. Kurt Tank, the designer of the Focke Wulf fighter aircraft, had worked in both Egypt and Argentina designing military aircraft to assist those that wished to bring about the demise of this Jewish State.

In Damascus members of the Muslim Brotherhood met with various individuals, some related to the South African recruited all those years ago and working for BOSS, Muller, now an elderly gentleman but with a history of SS membership that would make the Maquis of Sade appear to be a pussycat, plus Hamas leaders who were now responsible for all plans to continue the attacks against the population of Israel

An Islamic charity in Illinois, that on the back of property deals in the USA, supplied Hamas with funds for arms but had been busted by the FBI and subsequent to September 11, the various Arabian donors bank assets had been seized and frozen so funding was now a paramount subject. (*S.O'Neill now with The Times of London but then with the Daily Telegraph*)

The latest news at the Centre was that the main financial advisors had agreed to release funds to assist the fight but also concentrate on other issues.

During the normal monthly meeting at Inalco a stranger to the community entered the room. Frederick, who, as usual was chairing the meeting ,stood up.

"Gentlemen this is a very valued European member of our world-wide membership and will help us to achieve our aims, so let me introduce Herr Bruin,"

Bruin explained what he intended to do but emphasized the need to recruit more individuals in Europe who would fight the cause.

After the meeting ended Frederick took Bruin into an adjoining room where he told him that he was going to show him something special.

Frederick unlocked a door and they descended down a flight of stairs to a large chamber. He threw a switch and the chamber was suddenly lit with a number of wall lights revealing a room that made Bruin gasp.

The walls were decorated with highly polished wooden panels and above each separate panel were banners denoting various German SS regiments and famous Luftwaffe, Naval and Army units were displayed. At the end of the room were two framed oil paintings, one of Adolf Hitler the other of Frederick the Great.

Various paintings and pictures of various Nazi luminaries such as Goebbels, Speer, Doenitz, Heydrich, and Bormann adorned the walls. Glass cabinets displayed memorabilia such as medals, daggers and various awards. A large golden eagle with the Swastika underneath was affixed to the wall above and what looked like an altar there was a gold plinth which stood awaiting whatever tribute.

Bruin shook Frederick's hand, "Mein Gott, this is beautiful."

In the meantime and during the ensuing period Frederick maintained a strict control of the estate and started to implement the controls and edicts passed down to him by his grandfather and father as according to the legacy that they had left to him from all of those years ago in Berlin.

Bruin had by then returned to Europe where he monitored the activities of Mossad and the pro Jewish activists in Europe.

Organised bomb attacks on various Jewish targets throughout Europe were organised and the recruitment of new people prepared to fight for the cause. However there was a constant fight against the recruitment aims of the newer groups such as Al Qaeda but at a meeting in Beirut Bruin convinced both the Brotherhood, Hamas and Al Qaeda to work on a combined agenda.

Chapter Seventeen   Day Twenty Two   Chile/ Argentina

After yet another lengthy flight we arrived in Chile and made our way across the terminal to the desk where we would get the flight to Villa Baviera (Bavaria). On the way we picked up new sim cards for our phones and loaded them with local currency. I also booked a hire car that would be delivered to the hotel at the Villa Baviera.

A small six seater aircraft lay waiting on the tarmac Throwing our bags on board we took off, heading East for this strange destination on the edge of the Andes.

On landing a car from the hotel met us at the airstrip and took us to the camp. The scenery was certainly spectacular and was very reminiscence of Bavaria with a range of snow-capped mountains (Andes versus Alps came to mind) and we arrived outside a quite modern building. No sign of the barbed wire or watch tower,

The hotel manager met us and took us to the room he had arranged and requested that we dine with him and his assistant later that evening. After he left the room I telephoned Sammy and updated him on our contact details plus the meeting with the so called spooks at the airport in Lima.

We strolled down to the restaurant and sat down with the manager and his number two, a dark haired attractive woman who introduced herself as Inga Strauss, an Austrian lady who had lived at the camp for a couple of years.

We discussed the history of the camp and the bad publicity and I asked whether any of the old Nazis still resided at the camp. I was told just a few but if I was interested and wished to talk to these people that certainly would not be a problem.

After dinner we retired to our room and Rebecca looked quite concerned.

"OK darling what on earth is the matter? You look very unhappy."

"Harry, I have a very bad feeling about this place and the sooner you get whatever you need please let's get out of here."

"Fine, we will, just let me have a chat with these bloody Nazis tomorrow and off we go,"

"Inga wishes to show me around the facilities in the morning so hopefully we can sort all this out by tomorrow."

I pulled her close to me and my gut feeling was that something bad was about to happen and it made me quite sad.

"Darling I am so crazy about you and I am now getting a bit worried as well– so please cancel tomorrow's meeting and I agree let's fuck off."

She held me tighter and before I knew it we were on the bed exploring both our inner and outer bodies as though it was perhaps the last time we would ever see each other.

The following morning we rose early, packed our bags but after breakfast Inga turned up and before we could tell her we were leaving she took Rebecca's hand and they left together.

I was then introduced to a pair of geriatrics in the hotel lounge who had lived at the camp since its inception.

During these discussions I made out that I was an ardent supporter of the Nazi ideals and questioned them about funding and any neo-Nazi activity. Basically their answers were that they had received funding from Argentina mentioning Bariloche and a place called The Centre.

They also claimed that there was no neo-Nazi activity as they had left that to the Europeans but were confident that all would one day realise that Hitler's message was the truth.

They told me about a bank account that they used to receive benefits and make donations and one gave me the account details if I wished to make a donation but at the end of the day there was not a lot to take me further forward.

I returned to our room but no sign of Rebecca. An hour later I walked to reception and asked for Inga who said that a man had arrived an hour ago and met Rebecca at which time they had left in a car. I telephoned her but no answer.

Next call was to Mossad as it looked like the proverbial had hit the fan again?

Sammy called and I appraised him of the situation and told him that I was heading into Argentina into this place called Bariloche and that he needed to arrange some back up as I suspected that our German nutter plus an unknown number of extremists could be involved

Sammy said he would try to get back up from Beunos Aires and would be in touch with contact details. I suggested that to keep the whole thing on a need to know basis especially as we had not identified any leaks and that he alone should deal directly with Mossad.

The hire car had arrived so I told the manager that I wished to explore the area (I doubted that he believed that but to be blunt I couldn't care a fuck). On checking some local maps I saw that Bariloche in Argentina was not so far away the roads passing through the Andes.

A few hours later after driving through some of the most spectacular scenery I had ever seen I drove into the valley where the town of San Carlos de Bariloche was located. The name kept bugging me and then it came to me, yes this was the town that had been mentioned in the bloody book that I had picked up what seemed an eternity ago at Heathrow, Hitler's alleged bolthole.

Yes the buildings were certainly in the German alpine style and except for the road signs and advertising boards being in

Spanish I could well have been driving down Main Strasse Germany.

Now where the hell was Rebecca?

I checked my mobile and tried to trace her phone's location by her Sim card. Clever girl, the phone wherever it was now just some 40 odd few kilometres out of the town.

Right I now really needed a good plan of action, first to dump the hire car and get another one. So I drove to the new airport, dumped the car in the airport car park, walked into the terminal where I found Alamo offices and left the keys in the box provided , I then hired a 4x4 from Avis . While in the airport terminal I also found a list of local hotels and quickly located a place called Designer Suites in Bariloche which appeared very ideal as the rooms were self- contained and would offer good privacy.

I telephoned using a bogus name but booking in the establishment as an employee of a travel agency. A few minutes later I was at the suite and then telephoned Sammy and Mossad from the suite phone.

When I called Sammy, I told him about Rebecca's sim card location to which he replied that he would get some of his Government specialists on the case, with satellite surveillance of the location and all the technical gizmos they could use.

Whereas Mossad on the other hand told me that they had spoken to Sammy to appraise him of the situation and had agreed to supply the necessary back up that I needed. They also suggested that I should let their team take the lead on this development as not only did they want Bruin but also what secrets were being held in this "German Centre" in the valley. We arranged to meet at 10pm at my suite.

Chapter Eighteen   Day Twenty Three   Bairloche /Inalco

When Rebecca left the hotel nobody appeared to have noticed the fact that she was quite unsteady on her feet. Herr Bruin had in fact injected her and she was gradually slipping into unconsciousness.

The pair had arrived at Bariloche a few hours later but Bruin had not noticed that she had slipped her mobile phone down under the car seat cushions.

On arrival at Frederick's house Bruin carried her to a windowless room where he placed her on a bed strapping her hands to the bedstead. He then locked the door and entered Frederick's office.

"The Jewish bitch is upstairs and there is no doubt she will attract this bastard who has been working for the Jewish lobby and investigating our plans and financial wealth.

Within the next few hours there is no doubt whatsoever that this bastard will arrive in Bariloche and attempt to rescue her.

My contacts at Villa Baveira tell me that he hired a car and left the hotel several hours ago heading in this direction so once he gets here I will know and we will pick him up. My deep contact in Washington has also told me what the Jew loving scumbags are now upto."

"I hope Herr Bruin you are correct but we do not welcome failure so be warned."

Bruin's telephone rang and he was told that the hired car had been traced to Bariloche Airport and they were trying to see whether anyone had hired a replacement car at the airport.

"Shit, find out from the rental companies and the hotel booking phones where this bastard is "

An hour or so later Bruin's phone rang.

"Only three people hired cars today and we have traced two of them to a hotel outside the town and they are Brazilians. The third car was rented by an Englishman and we are looking for it now."

"Find the bastard now"

Meanwhile a local flight from Beunos Aires had landed at Bariloche Airport and four men walked through the entrance lounge and picked up a couple of pre-arranged cars then headed into town.

My telephone rang and a voice gave me a pre-arranged code word. I went down to the entrance of the hotel and I took the four men up to my accommodation.

After introducing themselves and exchanging pleasantries they suggested that I hid the hire car parked nearby so Benjamin left the suite and parked it some three blocks away removing the registration plates.

"OK Harry we have to work out a plan to get into Inalco and get Rebecca out of danger. While we are in the place you can get hold of any financial records and anything else to help our and your investigations."

"Fine but we should grab the computers of get someone to download everything they have including the deleted data,"

"Shit, where can we get that kind of expertise? Don't forget our main aim is to get Rebecca out of danger"

I made a phone call and confirmed that there was a computer expert in Beunos Aires who had the equipment to complete such a computer sweep.

"OK guys the equipment will be here in the next few hours and to be blunt we will be able to get everything from these arseholes computers which will satisfy both you and my client,"

"Great so let's now sort out our plan of action"

I said, "The best angle is that I act as bait, they do not know about you guys so you can come in on the back of me,"

"Harry that could be bloody dangerous, Have you any weapons?"

"Don't be daft but I do know how to use a gun,"

A revolver was then passed to me (a 9 mm Beretta Automatic with a nine bullet magazine)

It was agreed that I would visit the German school in Bariloche and hopefully the individuals at the Centre would be informed.

Meanwhile back at Inalco Bruin went to check out Rebecca.

"Tell me you bitch why I should not use you before I dispose of you and your stupid Englishman lover?"

Rebecca, struggling against the straps holding her down, saw Bruin dropping his trousers and seeing that she started laughing.

"My God you really are a dipstick, what are you going to try to do with that? It looks like a cocktail stick,"

Bruin hit her across the face, pulled up his pants and left the room.

A few hours later the Data Image Back System ("DIBS") arrived at the airport from Beunos Aires and I quickly gave the team a quick instruction on its usage. Quite easy really, just plug DIBS into the subject computer and the machine will load and copy everything from that computer's hard drive even the deleted files.

"How does it do that Harry?"

"Well I am not a computer expert but I understand that when a file is deleted and then written over traces remain on the hard drive so these traces can be analysed like a puzzle and by using key words the deleted document can be reconstructed. I used it a few years ago at an international electrical company where a director was selling trade secrets to the competition. The first document we found after just a few minutes was a memo he had sent to his, "clients."

A few hours later I left the hotel and headed for the German School, Instituto Primo Capraro.

I soon found the school (the town seemed to be full of educational establishments teaching every language known to man but German seemed to be the main language with many of the local shops selling German goods ranging from food to beers) which had obviously changed considerably over the past 50 years

Entering main reception area I approached the receptionist, a middle aged woman who looked up and greeted me in German. I explained that I was British and my family were arriving soon from Cologne and I was checking out prospective schools and a house to live in. She confirmed that there were places at the school and gave me some application forms to complete. As for houses she advised that there were a number of realtors in the town. I asked about the apparently very beautiful German settlement in a valley a few miles out of town as the family loved winter sports and it looks and sounded like an ideal spot. She replied that it was a very close community but she would go and speak to a member of staff who actually lived there.

Bruin's telephone rang and a short one sided conversation took place;

"The Englishman has just arrived I will try to keep him here."

Bruin immediately telephoned a small bar located near the school and instructed a couple of associates (actually off-duty policemen of German descent) to pick up the problem.

Meanwhile I had discreetly texted my Mossad back-ups who were sitting outside the school in two separate cars. One car left immediately and headed East out of Bariloche as after studying the maps of the area we were all aware that to get to The Centre, which was some 40 miles away as the Crow flies, it would be necessary to drive to the other side of Nahuel Huapi Lake, then take the road West along the North side of the lake heading for Villa La Augustura, the Centre being a few miles to the North of that town.

Sitting chatting to the receptionist I felt a hand on my shoulder. A short but squat individual smiled; "I believe that you are interested in properties in the Centre so Frau Holstein here has asked if you would like us to give you a tour?"

"Fine, shall we take my car?"

"Yes that would be good my friend." He turned to the other man who was slightly taller,reeked of tobacco who just nodded.

I thanked the receptionist and we left the school buildings and climbed into my car. The squat individual introduced himself as Alfredo and climbed into the passenger seat. The taller individual said nothing and sat on the rear seat. Pleading ignorance I asked for directions and Alfredo told me to drive East out of the town as we had to drive round the lake to get to the other side before heading West.

The tall man kept checking behind but the Mossad driver was using the method of driving ahead not behind and I noted that he had tied some skis to the car's roof rack. He therefore looked like yet another winter sportsman heading for the nearby Andes for a bit of ski-ing.

We soon were driving around the edge of the lake and then started to head West towards the Andes on Nationale Route 231. The scenery was spectacular with vast expanses of blue lakes and snow- capped mountains.

The road was steadily climbing and after quite a few miles with mainly light holiday maker traffic and just the occasional goods vehicle. We soon entered Villa La Augustura, drove along a wide garden centred boulevard then turned right to the North. A couple of miles out of the town I noted a small Restaurant named Parilla Chop Chop by the side of the road with the Mossad car parked in the car park.

I drove into the car park Alfredo asked me why I was stopping. I explained that I needed to go to the toilet and needed a coffee. They reluctantly got out of the car with me and we entered the restaurant.

We sat down at a window table and I ordered some coffees then rose to go to the washrooms. A few seconds after I entered them the tall silent friend of Alfredo opened the door and walked past the urinals towards the cubicles. He knocked the first door, received no answer and checked that it was empty. The second door he knocked and I replied. He pushed the door open and the Mossad agent shot him through the forehead with a silenced gun. We dragged his corpse towards the window, removed his documents, gun and mobile phone and then pushed his body through it where it dropped into some bushes growing below.

The Mossad agent returned to the dining area where he joined his partner and a few moments later I also returned. Alfredo looked toward the washroom door then at his watch.

I drank my coffee and told him that we should get on our way. He shrugged and went to the washroom door and shouted to his friend. On receiving no answer he looked quite bemused and ran into the room. A few seconds later he returned and I could see that he was not a happy man. He asked me where the man was and I denied even seeing him in the washroom. With that I paid the bill and walked out to my car. Alfredo decided to come with me and we were soon on our way but this time the Mossad car was some quarter of a mile behind us.

We arrived shortly after in this stunning valley and I noticed what looked like the ruins of a watchtower or castle rising out of the trees like a Bavarian medieval folly. Alfredo tried to telephone but it was apparent there was no signal.

The road had deteriorated into a track through the forest but suddenly the trees cleared to reveal an Alpine like meadow, with, what certainly looked like a Bavarian styled villa at the end of it, backed by a pine forest.

I pulled up at the front of the house, turned to Alfredo and asked if this was one of the properties that he wished to show me as it looked to be a bit out of my price range. He replied that it was owned by the local landowner who would have details of the available property to rent or purchase.

He left the car and spoke into an intercom at the front door. While he was out of the vehicle I hid the Beretta under the passenger seat up in the seat springs.

I left the vehicle and Alfredo beckoned me to follow him into the house. The entrance hall was wood panelled with game trophies and coats of arms shields hung at random. I noted at least two CCTV cameras placed strategically in the top corners of the hall.

A grey haired gentleman dressed in a dark green blazer, grey flannels and black brogues led us up the hall to a door which he first knocked and then opened. Alfredo beckoned for me to enter the room first and followed behind me.

The door closed and I felt the muzzle of a gun pushing into my back. I was then pushed to a chair in front of a large desk where I was shoved down into it. Another man entered the room from a side door walked quickly across to me and punched me on the side of my head.

"You Zionist, Jew loving bastard. I have really looked forward to this day and believe you me after I have finished with you and the bitch upstairs you will both be praying that you are dead. No chance, you will both suffer and when it is all over your final days will make you both film stars as a recording will be played on the Islamic television stations and circulated to those who support our restoration of the German nation's rights."

"You must be Herr Braun, the nutter from the mental hospital. Where was it Damascus, Gaza or those caves in the Tyrol?"

This comment resulted in another punch this time in the stomach as Braun hauled me up on my feet and with Alfredo dragged me out of the room, up a short flight of stairs and then into a darkened windowless room. (I always had a big mouth) The door slammed shut behind me.

Braun had returned downstairs where he turned to Alfredo and asked where his colleague was. Alfredo explained that they had stopped at a restaurant at my request where I had gone to the men's room, his colleague had followed me but had disappeared.

"Did you check to see if the bastard had a gun?"

"No Boss."

"Shit you had better get someone to check out the restaurant like yesterday and I'll have a look in his car. When you have made the call go up and ask the bastard what really happened at the restaurant – give him a bit of pain to get his memory restored."

Braun left to go out to check the car, Alfonso telephoned some associates in Villa La Augustura and instructed them to check out the restaurant. Then pulling a horse whip out of a cupboard went back up the stairs.

In the meantime I had found a light switch and turned the very dim light on to see exactly where I was. Not much furniture, a couple of wooden chairs, a table and a bed with what looked like a pile of blankets and clothes on it.

Suddenly the door opened and Alfredo appeared holding a horse whip. He lashed out stinging my left arm.

"Right you English bastard what happened to my amigo at the restaurant?"

I edged round the room although the space was rather limited and Alfredo was trying to catch me with the whip."

I suddenly noticed some kind of movement from the pile of blankets on the bed, Alfredo had also sensed the movement and turned to look at the bed. I quickly picked up a chair and hit him across the head. He dropped to the floor where I hit him again just to make sure he was not going to wake up in the near future. I turned towards the bed and saw this apparition come towards me.

"Rebecca. Did the bastards hurt you?"

I could see the bruises on her face and she appeared to be rather drowsy as if drugged.

I checked out Alfredo and found a 9mm pistol in his jacket, took out his phone which I smashed, grabbed Rebecca and we left the room.

Bruin was checking my car but had failed to find my gun but suddenly a rifle shot sounded the bullet smashing the door mirror of the car.

He crouched and started for the safety of the villa but half way there I appeared and when he saw the gun in my hand he climbed into my car and drove off with a number of rifle shots following him out of the meadow and into the trees.

Suddenly there was the unmistakable sound of rotor blades as a helicopter appeared above the trees, landed in front of the house, the other two Mossad agents with two other men had arrived.

The two with the rifles appeared out of the trees and we had a quick conference where it was agreed that the helicopter should be used to follow Braun and hopefully bring the bastard to justice. I told them that I was not sure whether he was armed or not but the vehicle had a tracking system and I suspected he would try for Chile.

We would remain, check out the computers, bank account records and anything else of interest.

The helicopter took off and we all turned to go back into the villa.

The old gentleman who had opened the door on my arrival stood in the hall.

"You have no right to enter this house. Please return from wherever you come from."

I held his arm and told him that any house where people were held captive by a murderer needed to be visited and the reasons for such kidnappings needed to be investigated.

I then asked him where the offices were and to take me there. Probably because of his age he complied and after passing through various well decorated rooms we were shown through a steel security door into what appeared to be the control centre of the house and estate.

The Mossad guys had the DIBS equipment and we prepared to open up the bank of computers.

Rebecca looked quite unwell so I led her across the room to a leather sofa and sat her down got her a coffee from a machine nearby, kissed her and told her to relax.

I then rang Sammy appraised him of the situation and asked him to get one of his computer experts on the phone in the event we were unable to open up the computers.

He asked whether if we managed to catch Bruin and where were we going to take him. I replied that this was going to be a potential problem as Bruin had now committed murders in the USA, the UK, plus kidnapping in Argentina and probable offences all over the place. We would have to wait and discuss that situation later.

We fired up the computers and with a little help from Washington DC we managed to get through the passwords and then make optical disc recordings of the hard drives.

As we were doing this a door opened and a gaunt figure entered the room.

Chapter Nineteen   Andes / Chile

Bruin drove like a maniac thanking the stupid Englishman for hiring a 4x4 as the roads up here in the Andes were at times very difficult to drive along. As soon as he could he would have to check out whether the vehicle had a tracking device fitted. After a few minutes he pulled the car over in the forest.

As he opened the hood to check out the fuse box and any electronics he could not hear any other vehicles although a helicopter could be heard in the distance. Finding the tracking device he disconnected the system and turned off the satellite navigation device.

He then drove off heading North for San Martin de Los Andes

A couple of miles back the helicopter was flying slowly above the forest but the occupants were finding it difficult to see anything through the covering of trees.

"It looks like the bastard has disconnected the tracking device and sat-nav. Try Harry's mobile which he left in the car."

"No signals up this bloody high"

"Radio through to control. Perhaps the Yanks can help out but in the meantime just let's keep our eyes open for a dark blue Mercedes."

Soon they were clear of the forest and flying along Route 234 surrounded by lakes and snow covered mountains.

There was no sign of the car whatsoever so they flew back retracing their flight path in case they had missed him.

Back on the ground Bruin had nearly reached San Martin de Los Andes where on arrival he planned to find some accommodation and hide the vehicle somewhere.

He found a Bavarian looking hotel (Hotel Caupolican) booked a room under a completely ficticious name paying cash, asked for a local street map and the location of the nearest shops, car hire agencies and left the reception area to purchase a few essentials.

The car was dumped in a local car park with the registration plates removed. After visiting a couple of shops he walked along one of the side streets and found the house in Cnel Diaz that he wished to visit. He rang the doorbell and an elderly woman answered the door.

"Frau Meissemburger, please read this letter. You will know who it is from."

She quickly read the letter and ushered him into the house. After pouring him a drink of schnapps she made a telephone call then smiled and told Bruin some friends would be here tomorrow.

Bruin returned to the hotel made a few phone calls from the public phone box, had a meal and retired waiting for tomorrow.

The helicopter had by then flown to the town but the Mercedes appeared to have disappeared into thin air.

The pilot decided to fly the 21 kilometres to the local airport and requested permission to land. When granted he set the Bell down by the small terminal building.

A chat with the local staff revealed that there had been no flights out that day by the local carrier LAN but the pilot was also advised that he should be very careful flying so close to the border as the Chilean Air Force did not like unauthorised aircraft entering their airspace.

A phone call was made back to control and it was decided to stay in the town for the night and see whether Bruin appeared as the town's closeness to the border with Chile was Bruin's best chance to get out of Argentina.

Chapter Twenty   Inalco & Frederick's Chamber

The gaunt man entering the room had a slight stoop and suddenly starting shouting, almost frothing at the mouth.

"What are you Jewish scum doing in this house?"

I walked across towards him and told him to behave himself and the best thing he could do right now is cooperate with the various agencies involved.

"What do you mean?"

"Well my friend at the moment your man Braun is wanted by nearly every law enforcement agency on the American Continent for murder, kidnapping, money laundering and probably every other crime known to mankind. Your involvement puts you in the proverbial frame as an associate so we need to know all about your operation. Either help of suffer the consequences of not cooperating."

Frederick sat down in utter despair, "What do you wish to know? You have got to understand murder, kidnapping? We are political and do not control extremists."

"Well Freddy let us talk. Tell me about your organisation."

"Well it is a long story and I will have to show you evidence to confirm this but to be blunt this estate has been the heartbeat, the core,the brains of setting up what people would call the Fourth Reich."

"The Fourth Reich?"

"Yes well as you may know many of the patriots including my parents fled Germany after 1945 to find a better life and think about our Fuhrer's ambitions."

"So what are you now going to tell us? The millions of gold and cash transferred to Argentina that was stolen from the Reich and others? The Nazi criminals living here in and working on the estate like Eichmann and Mengele."

"No, that was before my time although I did hear about it."

"Right let us talk about the money coming from here, where is it going and to what purpose?"

Frederick looked down and I watched his reaction. It looked like a long held dream was about to collapse.

"Freddy, I do not know what you may be on about but there is obviously something that is haunting you."

Again no comment.

Frederick stood up and I followed him to the door that he had entered the room from.

"You Harry are English and not Jewish?"

"Correct."

He unlocked and opened a door and we descended down a flight of stairs and entered a large room..

"My inheritance Harry,"

In front of me was this hall adorned with Nazi memorabilia, flags, photographs, regiment and unit regalia plus medals, weapons, and books. At the end was a kind of altar with oil paintings of both Hitler and Frederick the Great hanging on the wall behind this altar.

"Frederick, I have heard about this but why use this museum as a means to some distorted view of the world?"

Frederick pressed some hidden button and a shutter rose in the wall under the paintings. He walked towards it and lifted an object from the shelf within.

Spotlights came on shining on the golden plinth on what looked like an altar.

He turned and beckoned me forward. By this time he had uncovered the object. It was a skull.

The skull had been placed on the altar and I noted that precious stones had implanted into the bone structure.

"What the fuck."

"This is my great Grandfather Harry."

"Yes, but who are we talking about?"

"Mein Fuhrer, Adolf Hitler."

So this is where the skull ended up, now being used as some kind of God. No wonder the skull the Russians had was that of a woman.

I asked how it had arrived in South America and Frederick stated that it had arrived in U 530 with a special cargo in 1945. Apparently when Hitler committed suicide it was decided to ensure that nothing remained for the Russians to display and his head had been removed, placed in a lead lined box and transferred from Berlin to Argentina by air, ship and submarine. It was believed that his great grand- mother's skull had been recovered by the Russians who believed that it was Hitler's.

This was beginning to make sense especially the reports that the skull pieces the Ruskies had were those of a woman.

He then told me that his grandparents, with Eva Braun's orphaned son, had arrived from Germany shortly after and they had all lived in Patagonia ever since but the main ambition of those in the settlement was to revive the Nazi ideals.

I told Frederick that it was best to destroy the skull but he refused.

So this is what this was all about, the resurrection of the Master Race.

Rebecca appeared at my side and shivered.

"Harry, this was the bastard that murdered millions — what are you going to do with this place?

"Burn the fucking place to the ground, once and for all."

I took Frederick out of this mausoleum and re-entered the control office. The computer back-ups had been completed and the filing cabinets had been examined with relevant copies being taken of various documents

"OK Freddy we have seen the relics, have the computer stuff what else is there before we take this place apart?"

"That is your problem, not mine "

There was obviously something that needed uncovering.

The old man servant was standing like an obedient servant in the corner.

I spoke to one of the Mossad guys;

"Fuck it, shoot the old bastard preferably in both knees."

Frederick ran across the room screaming that we should not.

"OK Freddy, now shut the fuck up and tell me what we need to know before I burn this shithole down."

"The bunker, that's where you need to go."

We went down to a bunker behind the villa where we found a very secure semi-underground structure. Frederick opened a heavy steel door.

Inside the damp interior we found a large roughly lined hall but on wooden pallets were piles of gold bars. A quick check showed that they were stamped with the Nazi emblem and Reichsbank markingss. On other shelves were cases of paper money and gold coins.

"What the hell is this Freddie?"

"It arrived during and after the end of war years but we only use it when we really have to."

"What to buy groceries down the local Walmart or fund some extremist nutters?".

This was obviously the local's massive nest egg.

I rang Sammy and updated him on the local situation but did not mention the Skull and asked whether we could trust the local authorities or could we get a team down here to complete a deep cleanse of the place.

He thought the second option was best and confirmed that a team would be flown down within the next 12 hours.

In the meantime I arranged that Frederick and his family, after taking their passports away, plus the old gentleman, would be taken to Bariloche and secured in a rental apartment in the town.

I pulled him to one side;

" Look I cannot change your opinions but for you to go out there declaring your inheritance that will result in extremism, people being killed and to be blunt the Nazis were not political but no better than Al Capone and the Mafia.

All this gold was no more than loot stolen from the conquered peoples of Europe and those murdered in the gas chambers."

"What gas chambers? Many have told me that it is all a fabrication of the Jews."

"Freddy, please get bloody real. Look at the fat man Goering, bigger and fatter than a bloody Zeppelin. Did you know what was recovered from his house Karinhall and the mines where he stashed his loot? He made Shylock in Oliver Twist sound like a Saint."

"So what will happen to me and my family?"

"Well the biggest problem that you now have is that you associated with a murderer and kidnapper plus it is believed many of your organisations may be involved in the narcotic trade. If that is true, you could be ending up wearing not a brown shirt but an orange suit in some U.S. prison."

He and his family climbed into the cars provided and were taken away from Inalco.

We had a last search of the place and the Mossad guys left with the computer records and that left just me and Rebecca.

We entered the lounge area of the house where we quickly discovered a cabinet filled with wines and spirits.

Pouring two large malt whiskies I sat down with Rebecca on the large leather sofa, toasted her health and hugged her very, very, closely.

We did not sleep much over the next twelve hours and I knew that very soon I was soon probably going to have to say goodbye to this beautiful woman.

Chapter Twenty One   San Martin de los Andes

Bruin had awoken the following day and received a telephone call to his room at Hotel Caupolican and quickly met two Germans in the hotel lobby.

The Germans explained that they were going to take him to the local airstrip (airport) where they had booked him on a flight out of Argentina but not to Chile the nearest place but North so he could leave the continent undiscovered.

Bruin asked at what time to which they replied now. He left to get the few belongings he had and left the hotel with the men.

Meanwhile the helicopter crew and Mossad men had searched the hotels and local bars the previous night to no avail and had decided to sit on the airstrip to see whether the elusive Bruin turned up.

Bruin climbed into the German's car sitting next to the driver and they headed for the airstrip. Two miles out of town the passenger in the rear of the car pulled out a revolver and Bruin's brains ended up all over the windscreen. The two men dumped the car down a small ravine where it was set on fire and a few minutes later were picked up by a local Police car.

On their return to town they made a few phone calls to Washington DC.

Chapter Twenty Two – Argentina -Washington DC

I woke the following morning closely entwined with Rebecca and stroked her back until she opened her eyes at which time I kissed her gently after which we made love as though we had been apart for several years not a few days.

"Rebecca, what darling are we going to do now this is nearly over?"

"Harry, days with you could be boring but the nights would be beautiful."

I kissed her and laughed.

"OK let's just play it day by day, sorry night by night."

She laughed and kissed me very passionately.

On hearing vehicles arriving outside I jumped out of bed and saw that there were a couple of vans and a team of people who had obviously arrived to sort out the house.

Quickly dressing I went outside and met the manager of the team of people. After checking his credentials I took him on a tour of the place and instructing him as to what was to be removed from the house.

I instructed the manager of the team to clear the house room by room, put the furniture and the personal goods in storage in one of the barns, pack all accounting and office records including computers and take them to a secure warehouse in Bariloche.

A couple of armoured security vehicles hired by Uncle Sam had then arrived and the guards were instructed to immediately load the gold and monetary assets. On checking the inventory that Frederick had kept I ensured that what was loaded agreed to that record. The security vehicles were told to wait for my instructions.

The manager of the house clearance team asked me about the inner chamber I advised him that in exactly 12 hours the premises would be destroyed in an "accidental fire " so those artifacts within would be destroyed. He assured me that they had nearly completed the clearance.

I then instructed the security vehicles to drive immediately to Bairloche Airport where they would be met by U.S Government officials.

Rebecca asked about the skull to which I told her not to worry.

A few hours later a helicopter arrived and took us to Bariloche Airport. As we took off and flew across Nahuel Huapi Lake towards the airport I opened the window.

"Harry what on earth are you doing?"

"Just say goodbye to Adolf darling,"

With that I threw the weighted, with a lump of concrete, bag out of the window and watched it splash into the centre of the lake.

"You could have sold that for a lot of money."

"Not bloody interested – perhaps I can sell tickets for a treasure hunt. No darling, bollocks-good riddance to the shit."

(I did not reveal that I had taken DNA samples from the Skull. Frederick and others in is family)

We landed at the airport and Sammy was waiting in the departure area.

"Well done Harry, glad to see that you are OK Rebecca, come on you guys follow me. "

Sammy waved a pass at an Argentinian Customs Official and we walked out onto the tarmac where a U.S. Government chartered Boeing Airliner was being loaded with the gold and monetary assets taken from Inalco.

We climbed up the steps into the cabin where we sat down opposite Sammy and a bottle of Champagne was produced from the galley. The loading was completed and the aircraft began to move off the ramp. I looked at my watch.

"Sammy, ask the pilot to circle Inalco we might be lucky to see some pyrotechnics."

The pilot agreed and as we took off the aircraft circled low over the lake and towards Inalco. We all looked out of the windows as we flew across the forest and there was the villa and at the very moment we flew above it there was a blinding flash and flames started creeping up the walls of the house. Suddenly there was an explosion from the area where we had seen the Nazi inner temple and then we were turning North heading back to Washington DC.

Sammy looked at me;

"Harry was that a good idea?"

"Sammy if it had not been destroyed it may have ended up as a shrine for all the looney neo-Nazi nutters across the planet."

Sammy said that we were probably stopping for refuelling in Jamaica but would like to update us on some recent developments in Washington DC before we arrived back there.

"You were right about the leak Harry and it was from both my office and the CIA.

Let me explain, but first I have news about Bruin. He was eliminated by two contractors working for the CIA. Apparently after he fled from Inalco he drove up to a small town on the border with Chile, a place called San Martin de Los Andes where he contacted a German woman who had worked for the OSS at the end of the war. She immediately rang a CIA sleeper agent in Beunos Aires who contacted Washington. Now the bastards in the Agency have not told me this but while investigating where the damn leak was I found from telephone records that it was a member of my staff who was passing on information to an old FBI colleague who happened to be now with the CIA. Further investigations revealed that this CIA contact had met Bruin in Europe while Bruin was working with the BDO."

"So who was your leak Sammy?"

"You remember the guy who picked you up at the airport?"

"Not Joe?"

"Yes, you've got in one.

When he was in the FBI Joe and his friend were on the take with the Mob in Vegas but that stopped when their client was rubbed out.

By then Joe had got himself into considerable cash problems with the loan sharks and gambling so on speaking to his CIA partner they both came to an arrangement especially in connection to the Mexican drug cartels relationships with the Mafia.

When Bruin, who was by then free-lancing for the Brotherhood, had Rebecca's lot and your London client under surveillance , he contacted the old CIA friend with a good financial offer so Joe started passing all that he could get hold of back to Bruin via his CIA buddy."

"Has he been arrested?"

"No Harry he seems to have disappeared."

"So what's next Sammy? I plan to get back home as soon as possible tell the client what we have established and the fact that we have closed down one major source of funding and hopefully your lot can close down this hub bank and start freezing bank accounts where they have been used for both money laundering of drugs money and financing terrorism."

"No problem Harry but I would like to have a day just going through all the stuff we have so we can build on that and make the necessary arrests."

"Fine but I think Rebecca and yours truly would like to stay somewhere a bit peaceful for a few days so why don't you drop us off in Barbados and refuel this aircraft there? We can always set up a video conference from a hotel and by then Mossad will have analysed the computer records that we obtained from Inalco and of course the documents that we also seized."

Sammy looked disappointed but smiled and said that it made sense.

Rebecca then said;

"Harry, you have not told him what else you found."

Sammy looked at me.

"Sorry Sammy, Rebecca's talking about the mausoleum in the villa and guess whose Skull was displayed on what looked like an altar?

"How the hell would I know?"

"Adolf Hitler and the guy being held in downtown Bariloche is allegedly Hitler's great grandson."

"Shit – can he prove it? "

"Well I took some DNA from the Skull, Frederick and his family so we will have to check it out but to blunt it will probably be best if it's kept secret. Can you imagine what would happen if this news hit the streets? Every bloody nutter in these Neo-Nazi groups would be setting him up as some kind of Messiah."

"Where is the Skull now Harry?"

"Well Adolf decided he wished to go for a swim."

Rebecca and Sammy laughed and the two stewardesses entered the cabin and after pouring more champagne they asked what we would like to eat.

A few hours later we were woken as we approached Barbados and shortly after the aircraft landed at Grantley Adams International Airport.

Chapter Twenty Three   Barbados

Sammy had arranged transportation and after saying our goodbyes at which time he promised to get in touch and that he had booked and paid for us to have one of the rooms at the Sandy Lane Hotel.

The car took us to the hotel where we were greeted at reception and told that we had been booked into one of the Dolphin Suites and we were not to hesitate to ask for anything that we needed.

The suite knocked us out and the view from the patio of the azure Caribbean was mind blowing. On the table on the patio was an ice bucket, a bottle of champagne and an array of bottled spirits. Inside the suite there were vases filled with tropical blooms and baskets of fruit.

The next few days were so blissful I could have stayed there forever. Rebecca had recovered from her ordeal in Patagonia and the bruises on her face had disappeared helped by the beautiful sunshine and her tan was improving every day.

The telephone in the suite rang and Sammy asked how were enjoying ourselves and that he would like to have a video conference call with us whenever convenient. I told him that I would sort out one of the conference rooms at the hotel which I understood had all of the state of the art equipment that we would need and that I would ring him back confirming the time. I also suggested that he contact the

Mossad guys as it may be a good idea to have a three way chin wag. He agreed and hung up.

I wandered through to the bathroom where Rebecca was soaking in the large bath tub.

"Are you joining me darling?"

"I would love to but Sammy has just been on and wishes to have a conference call as soon as possible. I have suggested that he includes your colleagues in the call and I am just going down to reception to see what the conference room availability is like plus I need some cigars."

I gave her a quick kiss and went down to the hotel reception area where I managed to book a conference room for the following morning. However I did not wish to pay a second mortgage for the cigars on offer at the hotel so I returned to our suite telephoned Sammy giving him the time and the date of the proposed conference call. While talking to him I asked whether there was any news of Joe. Sammy said that he was still missing and that there was no sign of him at either his house or his regular haunts.

I asked about the CIA guy and where was he? Sammy said they are being pretty tight lipped and as they did not realise that he knew about this man's association with both Joe and Braun so he could hardly ask what was going on.

I agreed and said that I looked forward to our call tomorrow.

Rebecca appeared from the bathroom wearing a skimpy bikini with a sarong tied around her waist.

"Come on darling lets go into town this afternoon so I can get some cigars and see what the locals get up to. It will make a change from this luxury."

"Yes that will be great I would like to do a bit of credit card massacre."

A taxi took us into town and we were soon walking down Cheapside Street checking out the market and the little shops. This old colonial town was so very, very different from Bariloche. We ended up at the Jolly Roger Bar where a steel band was playing and calypso music filled the air. Rebecca refused to limbo and playfully punched me when I told her she was too fat.

We returned to the hotel and the telephone in our suite showed that there was a message awaiting me. I phoned reception and was told that there had been an urgent message from Sammy.

"OK Sammy what is going on my friend?

"Harry, bit of intelligence in respect of Joe. It looks like they fished a body out of the Potomac a few hours ago and we are waiting both the Police and Medical Examiner's autopsy."

"Any signs of cause?"

"No Harry we will just have to wait."

"What about his erstwhile friend over the park?"

"Nothing Harry, nothing whatsoever."

"Sammy let's talk tomorrow but I think it's about time you called the CIA's bluff. Hopefully we may identify a link with this scumbag with the drug money laundering."

Rebecca looked concerned and asked if I was OK. I squeezed her and told her not to worry although deep down I was concerned that there appeared to be a rogue CIA agent in operation out there.

We dined on the patio that night but I had this terrible sense of foreboding.

"Darling please smile you look like you have lost a pound and found a shilling."

"Sorry it's just we have been through a hell of a lot but there is still some bastard running free and if he is, as Sammy claims, allied to the mob there are going to be some seriously pissed off people out there. So the sooner I can get you out of harm's way the better."

"Harry don't worry about me I'm a big girl and don't forget I have some pretty awesome friends. So give me a kiss and let's enjoy these days."

I smiled, kissed her and poured a couple of glasses of a great white wine.

The following morning we went down to one of the conference rooms and after sorting out some coffee we awaited Sammy's call.

The call came through with a connection with Mossad and we looked at the images on the screens.

"Sod me Sammy for God's sake don't go into the movies you look like Jabba the Hut."

Sammy laughed; "Yes Harry I knew this was going to be a fucking mistake."

A voice broke into the conversation and introduced himself as Solly Silverstein and his first words were;

"You are looking good Rebecca."

She blushed and I nudged her which made her blush even more.

Sammy started the meeting.

" OK you guys let us see what we have; We know that the Cartels have been using charities including so called neo-Nazi groups to launder their narcotic income and the charities get their cut. Correct Harry? "

"Yes we have an apparent network of charity accounts being used to process income other than donations through a hub account in Mexico where the income is then split between dodgy Panamanian companies and offshore accounts in the Caymans."

Solly interrupted;

"Yes but the stuff we got from Argentina is mind boggling. Check out these flowcharts,"

He then produced a flowchart.

"Check this out guys. As you can see in the period 1944 through 1945 there was an amazing importation of funds into an account in Buenos Aires from an account in Zurich. This Swiss account appeared to have received funds from accounts through the Vatican Bank via Sweden but originating from deposits made by anonymous people who we believe were Nazis.

Now cross referring these deposits to the accounts held at the Reichbank in that period it is possible to confirm these deposits."

"OK Solly how does that bring us up to date?"

"Easy we have, as you can see from this chart, a flow of large amounts of monies out of this Argentinian account to Rio at the same time as the Perons were kicked out of power."

"So this Argentinian source bank account, whose was it?"

"It had a front name but the transactions were authorised by an employee of the Perons. By the way some of these transfers were from German companies such as Mercedes operating in Argentina."

Sammy spoke;

"This evidence is all very well documentated, Solly?"

"Yes Sammy and look at this, you can see that as we go through the following years we can establish that the funds continued to arrive in the Brazilian account even after the Perons had disappeared into history. We can see that monies were then transferred to accounts in Spain, Switzerland and Egypt during the 1950's and 60's."

"What do you think Harry?"

"Well this was all before any money laundering controls, the bloody Swiss were keeping their lips closed, and the masses probably could not have cared a toss. So let's bring all this up to date so from what you are saying the Mexican hub is a clearing house of both narcotics money and a mixture of Nazi loot, banking commissions for allowing charity accounts to be used, and transfers to dodgy cartel bank accounts, the Middle East and neo-Nazis "

Solly spoke;

"Yes you have summed it up exactly and obviously what interests us is the Middle East connection. That plus the elimination of the neo-Nazi funding is really going to make a difference. What about you Sammy?"

"Well the closing down of the hub will create problems for the cartels and no doubt they will move elsewhere their problem is they are going to have to find another charity to launder their dirty money. What we have to do now is not only freeze these dodgy accounts but decide what should be done with all of this loot confiscated a few days ago."

I butted in;

"Well as it was stolen from all over by the Nazis it will be impossible to compensate those losers so it may be an idea to use it to set up some kind of charity. This will or should be done with negotiation between various interested parties such as the UN, Holocaust foundations and whoever."

We continued to discuss this evidence for the next hour or so and then Sammy changed the subject to the latest news.

"OK Harry the body fished out of the Potomac was Joe Malone."

"So who is this arsehole over in the CIA?"

"His name is Benny Saprino, a third generation Italian descent American/Italian who joined NYPD before moving on to the FBI. Intelligence reports show that he was related albeit distantly to the Gambino Family and IA in New York suspected he was on the take.

As I told you recently Joe and this scumbag were involved with the Mob in Vegas probably with Saprino's connections and did pretty well. Then Joe joined us at the DEA with Saprino going to the CIA on a promise."

"On a promise?"

"Yes to avoid prosecution and set up a black operation in guess where? Argentina. During this period he travelled to Europe and was in Sweden when their Prime Minister was assassinated by, it is believed, the CIA assassin, Townley"

"Sammy this is getting more serious every bloody day. We now have a load of extremely pissed off Cartels, a nutter of a mob connected CIA agent who has just had his pocket money withdrawn and various individuals dropping dead like flies."

"I agree Harry everyone is trying to trace the bastard but he knows about you and Rebecca so I suggest you both disappear somewhere as soon as possible with no connections to anyone."

Solly interrupted;

"Harry you will probably be safe here in Israel and we certainly do not wish anything to happen to you or Rebecca as we like looking after our valuable assets. So if you wish we can sort something out over here."

I looked at Rebecca; "Sounds like we are on a round the world trip darling."

After arranging for all of this information to be passed to my clients in London we arranged to leave Barbados heading for Tel Aviv via Paris the following day.

Chapter Twenty Four   London

The following morning we flew out of Barbados with good old British Airways but again with different names. We landed at Charles De Gaulle and sat in the lounge waiting for the El Al flight to Tel Aviv.

"I'm not coming Darling. I have to sort these bastards out on my own turf with you well out of the way."

"No Harry what the bloody hell are you saying?

"Just this darling, please, please, listen to me, that is basically if anything bad happened to you I would kill myself. Just sit tight and hang on. "

I gave her a very long kiss and embrace and left the lounge picking up a flight to London City Airport.

An hour later I arrived at the airport grabbed a taxi and headed for Whitechapel.

Sod these bastards the East End was now in this war.

I was sitting in my favourite seat in The Blind Beggar (a notorious East End London pub where one of the infamous twins shot a certain gangster, George Cornell).

Author's note: was a great pub for sorting out late night parties in the swinging 60's and I used to sit on the barstool where Cornell sat on that infamous day.)

A couple of figures appeared through the door (Sod me in the light through the door (I could not recognise either of them)

"Harry you bastard where have you been mate,"

I grabbed his hand;

"Fuck me, where have you been you silly sod, still working at Billingsgate?"(*famous London fish market*)

"Yes you nutter, so what is taking place?"

"Well mate you really do not wish to know but what I do have it on good authority that someone from the States wishes to eliminate me."

I explained that I had upset a few scumbags and had rattled them big time. We agreed to set up a possible meet and I telephoned Sammy

"Sammy. it's Harry, leak some of this crap we have to those guys across the park and let it be known I'm in London."

A few hours later my phone rang and a voice asked for a meet at the Prospect of Whitby, an East End of London pub alongside the River Thames.

Later that same day I took a short taxi ride from The Blind Beggar to the Prospect of Whitby. As usual it was crowded with tourists and after picking up a pint at the bar I opened the door and entered the riverside terrace.

I found a table and awaited whoever. After a few minutes a guy sat down at my table and after exchanging pleasantries he, in an American accent, asked me whether I knew anything about South America.

Yes, I replied, I've just been down to Patagonia to which he replied you must be Harry.

"Yes I am Harry, who are you?"

"A very good friend of yours who would like to talk to you."

"A friend? I do not even know you. I can count my friends on one hand like most people but you, I cannot recall who the hell you are."

"Harry, do not be stupid. We should talk to stop what could be a problem to many especially to what is her name, Rebecca?"

"So that is what this is all about. You come here on my turf and threaten me and my friends. Who the hell do you think you are?"

"Harry, do not be stupid. You do not realise who you are dealing with."

"Sorry mate, meeting over, my friends will give you a lift home."

I put my hand up, signalling to my friends.

They came over and grabbed this messenger by the arms and they disappeared onto the Commercial Road and Whitechapel High Street.

I rang Sammy and told him to inform his CIA contacts to get lost and that one of their employees had just taken early retirement.

Interesting note: during 1943/5 thousands of tonnes of concrete were laid on airfields all over East Anglia. Post war much of this concrete was transferred to highway construction and during this period some criminals allegedly disappeared under such structures as the Bow Flyover.

Ginger Marks and the Bow Flyover comes to mind

Chapter Twenty Five   Conclusion.

Seychelles

Beau Vallon beach, Seychelles, a beautiful place with the warm Indian Ocean, white sands and exotic fruits. Yes there was the usual bunch of London taxi drivers with handkerchiefs tied to their heads and wearing socks under their sandals who spoilt the scene but then again, laying on a sunbed gazing over the blue sea, who wishes to look at others when one is looking in the eyes of a beautiful woman?

March 2014

Postcript

As this book is published two British newspapers have now, in the past few days, revealed the existence of a Nazi camp in Brazil during the war where the inmates had to salute Hitler; and the BDO have recently released files confirming a post war plan by SS officers to set up an organisation in East Germany to get rid of the communist yoke after 1945.

List of characters

Hitler and Eva Braun committed suicide in the Berlin Bunker 1945

Bormann` remains found in Berlin proved by DNA

Walter Schellenburg alleged lover of Coco Chanel, senior SS Officer but negotiated with many and tried to convince Himmler to overthrow Hitler (1910- 1952)

M.Quispemayta Peruvian Holocaust denier reported in 2012 and operated APNS.

Michael Townley Professional assassin working for the CIA and the Chilean Government murdering people in South America and Europe plus working on chemical weapons for Pinochet.

Colonia Dignidad Set up by Nazis in Chile and used for chemical weapon experiments for the Pinochet regime and allegedly include the Doctor of Death, Mengele and Townley. Paedophilia abuse as well.

U-977/U-530	Two German submarines that surrendered to the Argentine Navy in Buenos Airies July 1945. Details of their surrender have been taken from official records.
KG200	Specialist Luftwaffe unit that used captured aircraft for covert missions during the war.
Operation Kondor	The book, the Rebecca Code (the Germans used Daphne Du Maurier's book Rebecca as a code manual for covert espionage operations in North Africa) details this operation.
The Rest	All the other individuals as mentioned are ficticious except where I have stated certain facts as to the meetings as documented towards the end of the war and the alleged involvement by Dulles of the American OSS.

Reference Material

Although fiction I completed research and used the following books as part of that story. Obviously such websites as those detailing U=Boat activities, captured aircraft and campaign losses were examined so as to establish a basis of facts.

Armageddon   Max Hastings   ISBN 0 33390836 8

Nazi Gold   Sayer/.Botting   ISBN 0 246 11767 2

Donitz &the Wolf Packs

        B.Edwards   ISBN 1 86019 927 5

Last Days of the Reich   J.Lucas

Berlin   Antony Beevor   ISBN 0 140 28696 9

The Money Launderers

        Bob Blunden   ISBN 9781852525897

Wolfpack   Kaplan/Currie   ISBN 1 885410 630 9

Grey Wolf   Dunstan/Williams   1SBN 9781402781391

The Rebecca Code   Mark Simmons   ISBN 0752468707

Printed in Great Britain
by Amazon